Somebody's Someone

Nathan pulled Sabrina into his arms and close to his chest again. She caressed his face and toyed with his earlobes, clouding his mind. "I want you. But are you sure this is what you want, too?" His voice was husky with lust. He palmed the side of her face and peered into her eyes, which were full of longing.

Sabrina removed one of his hands from her face and kissed the palm. "I want you, too. It would be a crime to leave and not finish what we've started, don't you think?" Staring at him, her ebony eyes glimmered with desire.

Mesmerized by the promise he saw revealed by her expression, he lifted her off the floor and hurried off to his bedroom.

Once he arrived and laid her out on the bed, he turned on the light. He wanted to see her face, her every action as she responded to the heated rapture of their intimacy.

Indigo Romances are published by
Genesis Press, Inc.
315 Third Avenue North
Columbus, Mississippi 39701

Somebody's Someone

ISBN 1-885478-57-7

Printed in the United States of America

FIRST EDITION

Book Design by Mary Beth Vickers

Somebody's Someone

Sinclair LeBeau

Indigo Romances
Genesis Press

Dedication

With love to my husband, Edward, who is my romance hero.

To my dear sister, Rosalind Richter, my niece, Kathy Richter, my nephew, Alvin Richter, thanks for all your love and support.

To Sylvia Baumgarten, my editor, for being a joy to work with and challenging me to be a better writer.

And to my wonderful children, Ted, Kevin and Kimberly.

Sinclair LeBeau
P. O. Box 10262
Norfolk, VA 23513-0262

Prologue

"Hey Sweetness, can I go with you?" A young man in the crowded LaGuardia Airport Terminal stopped talking to his friend, smiled and appreciatively eyed the gorgeous young woman who walked toward them and right by him.

Sabrina Lewis tossed her hair and ignored their comment. She wasn't interested in the attention from the guys. Her mind was on her man, Malcolm, and making amends to him for neglecting him the last couple of months. The distance between them had placed a strain on her relationship. With Sabrina living in Hunter's Creek, Virginia and Malcolm living in New York because of his career, she knew that they both needed to have more patience with each other. Both of them had career ambitions that neither wanted to jeopardize. Sabrina had three business ventures that required her attention. She owned two beauty salons, Raving Beauty, a nail salon, Lovely Tips, and a glamour photography studio she had recently opened, which she had named Romantic Poses. All of these interests required her constant attention. And Malcolm had moved to New York with her encouragement and blessings in order to seek his fortune as a comedian/actor.

Strutting on high-heeled black boots with confidence and a glint of joy in her eyes, Sabrina thought of how great her life was going at the moment. In the last few months, her newest business, Romantic Poses, had done quite well. In fact, she was considering opening another glamour studio in the mall or maybe in the Virginia Beach area just outside of Hunter's Creek. Her shoulder-length raven hair was parted in the middle and had a soft sheen. Curled at the bottom, it bounced with each spirited step she took. Clad in a soft leather jacket to shield her from the chill of the October day, Sabrina hoped that Malcolm would be impressed by the sight of her in the bright orange silk shirt and matching slacks that complemented her complexion.

Outside the terminal, the night air was crisp and cool, abuzz with the hustle and bustle of incoming and outgoing travelers.

"Ride, lady?" A cabbie leaned across the seat of his vehicle and grinned at Sabrina.

"Yes, thank you." Sabrina smiled and walked toward the available ride. A nearby porter tipped his hat at Sabrina as he assisted her with her luggage. Seeing that she was settled in the back of the taxi and closing the door, the porter grinned and wished her a pleasant evening.

"Where to, lady?" the stocky cabbie asked. He peered at her in his rearview mirror.

Sabrina gave him the address of Malcolm's apartment, which was located in the East Village.

As the cabbie pulled into the confusion of the traffic, Sabrina palmed the sides of her face and yawned. She had gotten up early to check in on each of her businesses, to make certain that things would be in order and running smoothly while she took a couple of days off to put romantic harmony back into her relationship. It had been nearly six weeks since she and Malcolm had been together. After all the work-related stress she had endured in his absence, she needed to feel his arms around her, his body next to hers, comforting her in his special way. She felt a lurch of excitement at the thought of their bodies intertwined in raw passion.

"Hey, lady, are you somebody?" the cabbie asked, breaking the erotic fantasy that she had conjured in her mind. He stared at her in the rearview mirror with his brow furrowed as though he were trying to figure who she could be.

She chuckled. "I like to think of myself as somebody."

"Don't we all," he said. "But you sure look like one of

those television stars or a model. You're a good-looking woman. I was just wondering if you were somebody like that."

"I'm not somebody like that. I'm just a hardworking person like you."

He scowled at her in the mirror. "You had me fooled. I could have sworn you were somebody special."

"I'm somebody, but not the kind of celebrity special you're thinking of."

The cabbie shrugged, then turned his radio up while he made his way in the heavy traffic.

Sabrina settled back in her seat and pulled out her compact to check her appearance. This was a feat, since it was dark and she had to catch the occasional streetlights along their route. When she saw Malcolm, she wanted to look her best. She dabbed a touch of powder on her nose and across her cheeks and retouched her lipstick. Closing her compact, she thought of her last conversation with Malcolm—the angry exchange they had had. He had been disappointed when she had told him that she wasn't planning to make the stand-up comedy competition he was participating in tomorrow night. He had accused her of being selfish and only thinking of herself. He had told her how all of his friends in the business except him had wives and girlfriends who sacrificed their time to come out and show their support for their men. He had admitted to feeling lonely and defeated without her there to cheer him on. Sabrina had told him that she cared. But her life and job were just as important as his.

How dare he say she didn't care? she mused. She had accumulated phone bills with hundreds of dollars of long-distance fees with their calls to each other. She'd call him at the end of a long day to inquire of his progress with auditions and the comedy gigs he'd gotten.

"Here you are, lady," the cabbie announced, pulling to the curb of Malcolm's apartment.

Sabrina got out of the cab and stared up to the third floor. That was where Malcolm's apartment was located. He lived in the front part of the building. She saw no lights were on and worried that she had missed him. She assumed he had gone club hoping to check out other comedians who would be his competition. Maybe the idea of paying him a surprise visit wasn't such a good idea after all, she thought. Once he hooked up with his buddies from the clubs, he could be gone all evening, especially if they found a place that had an open mike night. She reached in her bag for her key-a key to the place that she rented for him.

Upon entering the darkened apartment, Sabrina expected silence to greet her. She was surprised to hear music playing softly on Malcolm's sound system. She flipped the button on the wall switch; she spotted two empty wine glasses and sniffed the aroma of extinguished scented candles.

"Malcolm!" Sabrina called, setting aside her traveling bag at the door.

Malcolm stumbled from his bedroom, tugging on his jeans. He stared at her as though he couldn't believe she was there. "Sabrina! I thought you...you had no time to come for a visit."

"I didn't. But I shuffled my schedule and delegated a few duties and here I am. I'm here for your special evening tomorrow night at that club." She rushed up to him, slid her arm around his waist to touch his bare flesh and kiss him. Her lips had barely touched his when she jumped back. She took the back of her hand and wiped her mouth, glaring at him. She smelled the fragrance of another woman's perfume. Her face crumpled with confusion. "Who is here with you?"

Before he could answer, she shoved him aside and stormed toward his bedroom.

Malcolm grabbed her by the arm to halt her. "Don't go in there!"

"Why not?" She shrugged off his grip and gave him a challenging look. Her stomach churned with anxiety.

Malcolm's brown complexion glowed with perspiration. His eyes shifted nervously.

Full of suspicion, Sabrina pushed open the closed door. Her eyes met those of a woman in Malcolm's bed. Her gaze swung to pieces of lingerie lying on the floor beside the bed.

4

The hussy cowered beneath the covers, giving Malcolm a questioning look.

"Oh no! How could you do this?" Sabrina's hands went to her face, which burned with humiliation.

The young woman pulled the covers up to her neck. "Malcolm? Who is this? What's going on?" she whined. Her eyes reflected her shame, her bewilderment. "What's she doing here?"

"Because I pay the rent. This is my place, too," Sabrina snapped.

Malcolm used his body to hustle an angry Sabrina out of the room. "Come on, Sabrina. Calm down. Let's go in the other room, so she can get dressed." He slammed the door to the angry insults of the woman in his bed.

"Take your hands off me," Sabrina ordered. She glowered at him. "You make me sick. I'm helping you to stay in New York and advance your career, and you're using this opportunity to screw around on me." Tight-jawed and trembling, she ran her hands through her hair. Her black eyes impaled him. Suddenly she lowered her hands and tugged off the precious diamond ring she had worn so proudly. With a look of pure hatred, she tossed it at him. It hit the floor in front of his bare feet. She leaned into his face, then whirled away from him and marched toward the front door. She grabbed her bag and slung the strap on her shoulder.

"Sabrina! Don't run out! Let me explain," he implored, stepping in front of the door to block her exit. "There's a restaurant on the corner. Meet me there. I'll get rid of her. She means nothing to me. Nothing," he whispered. He seized Sabrina by the shoulders.

She looked into his pleading eyes that almost never failed to captivate her, considering his suggestion. She wondered if it was worth her time to listen to Malcolm explain why he had to sleep with another woman when he was supposed to be in love with her-engaged to her.

She pursed her lips and heaved a sigh of exasperation. "Get the hell out of my way. It's over." She ground the words through her teeth.

The glimmer of hope that was in his eyes faded. Reluctantly he moved aside to let her go. "I wish you'd listen to me. I love you. I really do," he said as she stomped out the door and down the hall to the elevator.

"Stay away from me!" she shouted, glancing over her shoulder. "You'd better look for a day job. I won't be paying the rent here anymore."

She was thankful that the elevator doors opened the moment she pushed the button. She was greeted by the sight of two lovers, embracing and kissing. They paid no attention to her, but continued kissing. She stepped into the elevator and pushed the button for the ground floor. She turned her back on the ardent lovers and lowered her head. Tears poured down her face and a feeling of despondency consumed her. When the doors of the elevator opened, she lifted her shoulders and held her head high. She couldn't wait to get back to Hunter's Creek and the businesses. They would occupy her mind and smother the disappointment in her heart.

Chapter One

Nathan Atkins arrived at his friends, the Masons', New Year's Eve Party with the intention of having a few drinks and sharing a few laughs. He hadn't expected to find Sabrina Lewis at this gathering. He thought Miss Lewis would be off in New York in Times Square, celebrating with her hot-shot boyfriend whom he had heard she had. Nathan had met Sabrina at the Hubbard Community Center. She had come to the Center as a volunteer—a mentor for the urban teen girls. Charm classes had been her thing as well as organizing cultural events.

Ordinarily, he was annoyed by Sabrina and her "I am somebody better than you" attitude toward him. She had come to the Center and attempted to overshadow the work he had done with the kids.

Once she arrived on the scene, she let him know that she thought his use of sports to mentor lacked creativity and certainly wasn't anything that the kids could use in the real world. He had become offended. He prided himself on what he had done. He had gotten the kids in the community off the streets and kept them out of trouble. As a police officer, he knew how important it was to keep idle kids busy. However, "Miss Somebody" hadn't been impressed. Black kids needed to know more than sports to succeed, she had told Mrs. Blanton, the director of the Center. Sabrina laid out her fancy ideas for an after-school program she believed would be more beneficial. She wanted to see the kids in the community become well-rounded in different areas, not just athletics.

7

Sizing up Sabrina across the Masons' living room, Nathan saw that Sabrina looked fabulous as usual. Despite her snooty attitude, she was the kind of woman who could make a plain white t-shirt and blue jeans look terrific. Tonight she was a knock-out in a red mini-dress that complemented her petite yet curvaceous figure. She wore matching high-heeled pumps with ankle straps that showed off her shapely legs. She was sexy. She alerted every fiber of masculinity in him. He sipped his drink to cool his thoughts. He tried to ignore her, but it wasn't easy. Her hair was worn loose and combed to the side, covering one eye. Her flawless bronze complexion reminded him of tea poured over ice; it had a rosy tinge that caused his fingers to itch to feel its texture. He wondered if it had the dewy feel of a fresh rose. Sabrina could have been immortalized on canvas, he mused.

But tonight he was affected by her demeanor even more than her beauty. He saw the forlorn expression she wore when she thought no one was watching her. That lost little girl expression touched him, made him want to comfort her. However, he dared not act out his thoughts to Sabrina. He knew she was edgy, sensitive. She had too much pride to admit to needing a comforting word or someone to discuss her problems with. He had this gut feeling that her love life had gone astray. If there was one thing that he recognized, it was a broken heart. He'd been there. He knew all the signs of disappointment and of dreams being shattered. Nathan wondered where the man in her life was-the out-of-town lover who had always kept her from accepting a date from the available guys in town.

Nathan's evening-long fascination with Sabrina was interrupted when the robust guests roared into shouts of the countdown for the new year. "Seven, six, five, four, three, two, one...Happy New Year!"

Though Sabrina had come to the party alone, she had made

herself have fun. She'd had plenty to drink. She had danced and laughed a little harder and a little louder than she normally did. Her mission on this holiday evening was to drown the sorrows of her broken heart. The champagne had done a sufficient job of anesthetizing the pain. But at the stroke of midnight and the beginning of a new year, Sabrina could feel her facade crumbling. She had had enough of pretending that all was right with her world. She no longer felt like dancing or talking to anyone.

Alienated by the revelers, Sabrina tossed back another glass of champagne and decided to leave the party soon. A magician with all of his tricks couldn't turn the evening into a festive one for her. She'd had enough of the holidays. Ever since her trip to New York in October, she had fought to smother the pain and erase the images of a love gone wrong. She didn't want anyone to know that Sabrina Lewis was vulnerable. She'd always given everyone the impression that she was strong, tough.

Sabrina caught a glimpse of Nathan Atkins across the room. Tonight he seemed to stand out more than usual. The bright blue sweater he wore showed off his fine physique. He looked rather sexy. She shifted her attention away from him. She definitely had had too much to drink, she figured. She certainly didn't want to find anything of interest in Nathan or any other male. She heard several outbursts of laughter coming from the small group that was enthralled by Nathan's conversation. Out of curiosity, she returned her attention to him. A smile lifted the corners of her mouth in spite of herself. The Nathan she was seeing this evening was in no way just an ordinary man. Tonight he appeared to have a glow that set him apart from the crowd. Until tonight she had not noticed the way his caramel complexion magnified his large, hypnotic, hazel eyes, and the way his handsome square face beamed with a warm radiance that was alluring. She blinked her eyes to rid herself of the trance. She mustn't allow herself to be charmed. No, not again and especially not now.

Sabrina held out her glass to be refilled by the caterer.

Sipping on her freshened drink, she overheard two women discussing New Year's resolutions. One resolved to lose weight, while the other resolved to return to college to complete the degree she had abandoned in order to get married years ago.

If only her own life was as simple, Sabrina thought. She finished off yet another glass of champagne. No more romance. That was her resolution. At thirty, she believed it was time to give up on romance and relationships. A woman didn't need a man to survive. She hadn't known of anyone to perish for the lack of companionship. But she certainly knew plenty of good women who had been nearly broken emotionally, physically and financially in order to hold on to the illusive ideals of love and romance.

"Sabrina, can I have a kiss for luck for the New Year?" Nathan Atkins asked in a cheerful tone.

Sabrina had been lost in her cynical thoughts; his unexpected appearance startled her. Nathan stood close to her, smiling like a mischievous schoolboy. Unlike the other men, who had come to the party dressed in suits, Nathan was in jeans and a sweater. He had caused quite a stir when he arrived earlier, she remembered. Several of the guests had gravitated to the police officer who'd done a heroic deed only a few days before. They had congratulated him on the instrumental part he had taken in a hostage situation that had involved a distraught father who had held his wife and children at gunpoint. Nathan had managed to talk the troubled man into giving himself up without anyone being hurt. That was really big news for the otherwise quiet, yet growing town of Hunter's Creek.

Sabrina had watched the television news and listened to Nathan being interviewed by the media. He had come off as interesting and compelling. Though she hadn't bothered to really get to know him personally at the Center, he had gained her respect professionally for his dedication to the kids and for the way he handled himself as a police officer. He was a black man who had garnered respect.

"A kiss," she said. She forced a smile and reluctantly offered her right cheek for a chaste peck.

"Sabrina, come o
do better than that," h
excuse to get close t
the "Ice Princess." H
old man getting a fav
to taste her generousl
teasing. He guessed tl

Eager to satisfy
Sabrina's waist and p
upon her lips. The mo
his lips to her, he felt
thought with pleasure.
His heart swelled wi
enchantress, he decid
wanted the spell he had fallen under to last.

stirred in her.
"Thank you for your g
they aren't heartfelt." H
assumed a casual po
She shrugged
a fresh glass
approached
Nathan
perp

For a moment, Sabrina's eyes couldn't conceal the unexpected thrill she had received. She pulled away from him, gasping with indignation. In her struggle to free herself from his embrace and the effects of his sweet kiss, she managed to spill the remainder of her champagne on her voluptuous cleavage, which peeked out of the low-cut dress she wore. "Atkins! Watch it!"

"Oh, I am," he said, checking out the glistening mounds with a wry grin. "I'm sorry. I was only trying to share a little holiday cheer." He reached in his back pocket and pulled out a white handkerchief. "Here, let me do the honors." He attempted to wipe away the moisture.

"No! I've got it," she said, panicky as his hand went near her breast. She used her cocktail napkin to absorb the mess.

"Well, Happy New Year." He winked at her, chuckling with satisfaction.

"Yeah, whatever," she said unenthusiastically. She fought the urge to wipe her lips and erase the spark she'd experienced. The nerve of him, she thought. She wasn't in the mood to flirt. And especially not with Nathan Atkins. He had probably forgotten what it was like to be with black women. The negative thought served as the perfect antidote to the feelings he had

ood wishes, even though I can see
...e thrust his hands in his pockets and
...e.

...nd dismissed his presence. She reached for
...f champagne from the female caterer who
...her. She sipped on her drink and wished that
...ould vanish instead of watching her as if she were a
...rator he had spotted to nab for arrest.

"How about a dance? This is a party, a celebration."

"Listen, 'Sunshine,' don't concern yourself with me. Go find someone who is more your type to dance with. I'm not in the mood to dance with you," Sabrina said in a slurred tone. She ran her fingers through her lustrous raven hair and blinked her eyes. She could feel the effect of her drinks-dulling her senses, making her aloof.

"Are you all right? Can I get you a cup of coffee?" Nathan asked. "Too much holiday cheer, huh?"

"I don't want anything. I'm leaving. I've had enough of this house party." She finished off her drink, licked her lips and smacked them. Her eyelashes fluttered drowsily. She handed the empty glass to Nathan. "Top quality champagne. If it hadn't been for that, I would have left hours ago. Hey, I might not even have come." She laughed cynically. "But Kathy Mason kept bugging me. She said no one should be alone on New Year's Eve," Sabrina said bitterly. She eyed Nathan, who listened intently, and silently cursed herself. She had said more than she cared for him to know. She felt like a fool for talking too much. Hadn't she boasted to anyone who would listen that her man was everything a woman could want? He lived in New York and was an aspiring comedian who was destined to be a superstar, she'd bragged.

"Don't tell me that your superstar has deserted you on such a special night." Nathan smiled wryly as though he couldn't resist the jab.

Sabrina winced. She hated the fact that she had left herself open for Nathan, of all people. She figured he would enjoy taking her down a peg or two for the way she had overshadowed and even belittled his ideas at the Center.

"Brother man didn't have a big gig in L.A. or New York, huh?" He stared at her to see what lie she would come up with to cover up what she had revealed. Suddenly it was clear to him why she was downing so much champagne. Obviously, there was trouble in paradise. The only thing that would make a classy number like Sabrina lose her dignity was a broken heart, or a sorry man, he deduced.

She glared at him. "And where is your date? Shouldn't you be by her side instead of getting in my business?"

"I don't have a date. I've just gotten off duty. I dropped in here on my way home to catch a little holiday cheer before heading home." He stood with his arms folded across his well-defined chest. His stance was one that she had seen him assume when he was on duty as a police officer. "Too bad your man couldn't be with you. If I had a woman as fine as you, I'd have her with me wherever I was. Especially tonight," he added softly, squeezing her chin. "You've heard that old folk tale that the person you're with on New Year's is the one you're with for the rest of the year, haven't you?" He chuckled. "You could get lucky and wind up enjoying me for the rest-"

His touch was tender. It unnerved her. "Please." She shifted her head to shrug off his touch and rubbed her chin where his fingers had been. "Look, I'm going. Don't waste your charm on me." She was annoyed with herself for having enjoyed his kiss, his touch. "It's not working. I've had enough of this party and you." Despite her firm words, she couldn't move from the spot where she stood. She wished she hadn't had so much to drink. She stared at him, blinking.

"Don't go yet. If you do, the party will be over," he teased and grinned. "The party is just kicking off. Stay and share that 'charming' attitude of yours with me. Everyone here appears to be pairing off like they were on Noah's Ark." He raised an eyebrow superciliously and smirked at her. He stared into her ebony eyes in an attempt to persuade her. "Have some coffee with me. Let's get something to eat. The caterers are whipping up delicious omelets and biscuits as we speak."

Since she had been drinking and was a little tipsy, he hoped to entice her to stay and to eat. Though she had aggravated him with her bad attitude, he didn't want to think of her attempting to drive home in her inebriated condition. Hopefully, he'd get some coffee into her to sober her up. He hated to imagine her getting into an accident and endangering her life over some clown who evidently couldn't care less about her.

Sabrina wasn't in the mood to chat—to be sociable. "I don't want any coffee and I don't have an appetite for any food. Nor do I want to dance." She gave him a challenging look. "Go on and find someone else to entertain you. There's Becky McGregor over there and Lizzie Hoffman." Her expression grew implacable. "Both of them are more your type anyway, aren't they?" she asked caustically.

Nathan's gaze swung to the other side of the room where the brunette and the blonde white women who worked with Kevin Mason at the high school stood talking to Kevin and his wife, Kathy—the host and hostess for the party.

"My type? What are you getting at?" His voice carried an edge of indignation and he gave her a piercing look. "I happen to know both of them and they're two very nice ladies. I chose to spend my time with you and not them."

Nathan wasn't as naive as he pretended. He knew where she was coming from with her comment. It irritated him when black women labeled him a traitor to his race because he chose to date women of different racial backgrounds. As far as he was concerned, all women were the same whether they were black or white. He dated women based upon their personalities, their intelligence. The way he judged most people he associated with.

"Yeah, I bet." Sabrina's voice dripped with sarcasm. She glared at him. "Nathan, everyone knows that you have a preference especially for their type. You're nothing but a 'Crossover Brother.'" She looked satisfied with the verbal blow she had hit him with. "Don't look at me that way. You shouldn't be ashamed of what you are." She smirked.

The warmth in Nathan's eyes faded. He shoved a hand in the pocket of his pants and rubbed the back of his neck with the other hand to quell the irritation that roiled within him. "Is that supposed to be an insult? If it is, you've failed." He gave her a scorching look. "Yes, I happen to date some women who are white. But I like all women," he said in a defensive tone.

If he had any sense, he would walk away and forget "Miss Somebody"—Sabrina Lewis. But he sensed that beneath Sabrina's haughtiness there was a scared, hurt, sensitive woman. He had witnessed her working with the kids at the Center. She communicated with them quite well. He had a feeling that she had experienced some of the grim things that the Center kids had, and that made her even more of a curiosity to him.

Suddenly it was clear to him why she hadn't opened up to him since she had come to the Hubbard Center. Her vile comment made him understand why she wasted little of her time or conversation on him. She was one of those sisters who treated him like a pariah for being color-blind. He could never understand why black women took such a situation so personally. Didn't they realize how racist this attitude was? he mused. He had figured a businesswoman like Sabrina to be more open-minded and more intelligent in dealing with such issues. She couldn't afford to be racially biased. She worked with people of all races. He knew she even had white friends whom she socialized with on a regular basis. He couldn't understand why she had made such a big deal of attacking him for dating white women. Could that great boyfriend of hers have left her for a white woman? he wondered.

"I like all women." She repeated his words in a mocking tone. "I expected you to say something like that. That's the kind of thing 'Crossover Brothers' say to keep from offending us. Sisters know what the real deal is. A white woman makes you feel like you're above anyone else. You feel as though you've won a trophy with that white woman clinging to your

15

side. That's the attitude that sickens me." Sabrina glowered, then shook her head to ease the drowsy feeling she had from the liquor. To her chagrin, Nathan didn't storm away. She had been sure her comments would cause him to get as far away from her as he could.

He looked at her pensively. "You're wrong, Sabrina. I'm not going to discuss this with you in the shape that you're in," he said. His voice was a lifeless monotone. "You've had too much to drink. No need to be angry at me because your man has dumped you and you're miserable."

Sabrina's eyes flashed with outrage; she pulled her shoulders back. "My man has not dumped me!"

"Yeah, right," Nathan responded in a patronizing tone. Her reaction had proven that he was right. She wouldn't have responded the way she had if he hadn't hit a sore nerve. He liked the control he now had, knowing her secret. "No need for you to sink into a funk, Sabrina. You don't have to be lonely, sweetheart. I'll be more than happy to show you a good time."

"I'd rather be lonely than go out with a brother who is not 'real.'" She gave him a dark, smoldering look to hide her secret fear of not finding a good black man to fill the lonely void in her personal life. The older she got and the more successful she became, the more her search for a decent man looked grim.

Nathan's nostrils twitched at her insult. Black women and their bad attitudes. It seemed you could never do anything to please them. And he had stopped trying. He remembered when he was a young man who wanted the attention of the great looking black girls he knew. Gathering up his courage, he'd approached several of them for dates. They had laughed at him for daring to think they would even consider wasting their time with him. He was often told to his face that he was too nice, didn't wear the right kind of clothes or had no fancy car to chauffeur them around town; some people had even dared to tell him he acted white because he didn't use slang like the other black kids, but spoke in correct English. None of them would even consider going out with him to the movies or for a bite to eat at the mall. It was with his female white classmates that he had found companionship—the attention he needed from a female. They didn't make him feel like a social misfit, and white girls were more than eager to discuss class assignments or plans for college. They didn't think he was weird because he loved reading, watching independent artsy movies, and listening to all kinds of music other than rhythm and blues.

"Listen, you need to be careful what you say," Nathan chided. "You've got too much going for yourself to be speaking this way. If anyone suspects you might be racist you could lose a lot of friendships and business. The white community supports you and has been good to you. Be careful what you say."

"Racist? I'm not a racist." Her face crinkled with confusion. The issue she had brought up had nothing to do with contempt for whites. To her it was a relationship issue between black men and black women. Nothing more.

"Sabrina, let it go for now. We'll talk about this when you're more coherent. I'll get that coffee, so you can sober up before your mouth ruins you."

"Forget you, Nathan! Go get yourself some coffee. Or better yet, go serve some of these white women here. Maybe you can get lucky with them before the party is over."

"Sabrina, why are you attacking me?" His voice revealed his censure. "I've done nothing to you except try to be sociable. Friendly."

"I don't want to be sociable with you. Just leave me alone! I'm getting out of here. That's what I should have done a long time ago. I've wasted too much time with you." She opened her purse and fumbled for her car keys. "I'm sick to death of men. Dating," she mumbled. "It's nothing but a waste of my good time. Work and money are the only things that can guarantee a woman satisfaction." She snapped her purse shut and waved her hand in frustration. She shot him a venomous look as if he was responsible for all the men who had given women

17

grief in their romantic relationships.

Nathan was concerned by how flustered Sabrina had become. Beads of perspiration glistened on the tip of her nose. He had to stall her. She would be a menace on the road on the way home.

Catching him watching her, Sabrina turned her back to him. Suddenly, the room spun around her and she clutched her purse to her churning stomach. She slapped her hand over her mouth as she felt bile rising in her throat. She turned back toward Nathan and nearly knocked him over as she wobbled toward the bathroom.

Seeing that Sabrina was ill, Nathan took off behind her. But Kathy Mason appeared and intercepted him. He was relieved to see Kathy coming to her friend's assistance. Sabrina would probably resent him seeing her puking up her guts.

Even though Sabrina had made those disparaging remarks to him, Nathan knew that wasn't the real Sabrina. That was her hurt combined with the excess of liquor she'd drunk. She wasn't a mean-spirited woman. And she had a right to her opinion. But she had no right to attack him or call him names. So she didn't care for him, because she knew he dated white women. In spite of her opinion about him, she was quite a woman to admire and a good Samaritan as well. As a police officer, he had learned of the good things she had done for people who were down on their luck. She often contributed money, clothes and even free haircuts and hairstyles to women in homeless or battered women's shelters to enable them to feel better about themselves. Her assistance had managed to give them that chance they needed to look nice for a job interview that could give them the opportunity to begin again. And when school had opened in September, she and her staff had offered free shampoos and hairstyles to the young girls whose parents didn't have the money for such things. And in the last few months, she'd started volunteering her time at the Hubbard Center. She was a jewel of a woman for someone as young as she was. Her values weren't as shallow and superficial as many young women who were self-absorbed and concerned only about material things or partying their lives away.

In the last few months, when she had come to work at the Center in their mentor program, he had seen where her presence had made a difference. She had made quite an impression on the young, tough girls there. She'd managed to gain their confidence. This was a big step in helping them to alter the bad attitudes and the feelings of helplessness and hopelessness some of them had. He had seen the way the girls admired her well-groomed appearance. He heard the girls talking about how well paid she was, and how she made more than any men they knew her age.

Nathan watched the hallway down which Sabrina had disappeared to get to the bathroom. He wondered if she was okay. He also wondered what that creep of a boyfriend of hers had done to make her drink beyond her limit.

After about twenty-minutes, a pale-looking Sabrina emerged with Kathy at her side.

Nathan rushed over to her. "Are you okay?"

Sabrina wouldn't look at him. "I'm fine. Really. Thanks," she said softly.

"I tried to get her to lie down and perhaps stay the night here. But she won't have it. For some unknown reason, she is determined to go home," Kathy explained to Nathan. She frowned with concern.

"She's not in any shape to drive," Nathan said.

"I was going to call a taxi. Okay?" Sabrina blurted. "And don't talk about me like I'm not here."

"You won't need a taxi. I'll see to it that you get home. I'll drive you," Nathan volunteered. He placed a comforting hand at the small of her back.

"Oh Nathan, that's sweet of you," Kathy said.

"No, it isn't!" Brushing his arm away, Sabrina shook her head at him. "I don't want him to take me anywhere," she snapped. "I have no patience for black men like you who don't find beauty in their own women." She scowled at him . "Call me a cab."

"Sabrina! That's uncalled for," Kathy chided.

"It's okay, Kathy." Nathan shook his head at Sabrina's actions and shrugged his shoulders at Kathy. "Look, Sabrina angel, ease up on me. You're going to hate yourself in the morning when you wake up and find out that you dropped that cool facade of yours. And I'll be your whipping boy, if that's what you need for tonight." He smiled wryly.

+ Scowling, Sabrina whirled away from him too quickly. She reeled on her feet and stumbled sideways.

Nathan opened his arms and caught her. "See how handy I am? You just proved that you need me." He chuckled. "I'm seeing you home, lady. I'm starting the new year off right. I want you to see that I have a big heart and that I forgive all the rude comments you've made to me. Sit down for awhile." He placed his hand around her waist and eased her into the nearest chair. "I'll go get you a cup of coffee and then we can be on our way."

"Good. I'll guard her," Kathy told Nathan.

"Don't let her get away." He eyed Sabrina, who sat slumped in the chair. "She's a live wire tonight."

"I won't," Kathy said, taking a seat on the arm of the chair with her friend.

Although Sabrina wasn't pleased with the way she was being ordered around, she didn't argue. She knew they meant well. And she felt too bad to protest anymore.

"Sabrina, what's up with you?" Kathy asked. "You don't usually drink like this. I've been meaning to get up with you, but every time I was ready to get with you, someone new arrived and had to be welcomed." She rested her hand on Sabrina's shoulder. "I did manage to catch a glimpse of you a couple of times. You looked like a little girl who'd lost her favorite puppy. I invited you here tonight to have a good time and to forget your problems. Forget Malcolm Knight." She stared at her friend. "You look beautiful, but I suppose you scared away any potential male prospects with that evil look in your eyes."

Sabrina gazed up at Kathy and sighed. "I don't care. I'm

not ready to waste my time dating." She fidgeted in her seat. "I've tried to be strong, but I just can't seem to get the image of Malcolm and that...that woman out of my mind. I try to stay busy. I keep telling myself I don't need him, but...I still hurt, Kathy." Her voice broke with emotion. "I told you I wasn't ready to come out tonight. And I used Nathan as my scapegoat. For some reason, he just wouldn't stay away from me. He got on my nerves and I was awful to him. Do you think he'll dump me on the side of the road for the way I've talked to him?" She hung her head in misery.

"Don't be silly. Nathan is a good guy. I know it's been hard for you. These men are too much. They just don't know how to appreciate a good woman." She squeezed Sabrina's shoulder. "They're always complaining how sisters don't understand them and don't know how to support their dreams. Here you have supported that Malcolm financially and emotionally, so he could live in New York to get this comedian thing going. And what does he do? He stabs you in the back by having some wannabe actress living with him as his lover and at your expense. It's disgusting."

Sabrina lowered her head and let the tears she had been holding in all evening spill from her eyes. "I was a good fool, wasn't I?" She attempted to laugh through her tears, but she failed. The tears still flowed.

Kathy handed her a napkin from a nearby table to wipe her eyes. "Go on and cry, sweetie. No need to keep it all bottled up, girl. You've been working extremely hard so you wouldn't have to deal with your heartbreak. Your emotions. Now it's caught up with you. The liquor made you even more melancholy." Kathy patted Sabrina on the back and whispered in her ear in an attempt to cheer her. "I saw Nathan flirting with you. I caught him sizing you up several times during the evening. He even cornered me to ask what was bothering you."

"You didn't tell him anything, did you?" Sabrina dabbed away tears from her mascara-smeared eyes. She didn't want Nathan or anyone else in Hunter's Creek, for that matter, to know what a shambles her private life was. She figured people wouldn't respect her professionally if they knew she couldn't even hold on to her man.

"Here's that coffee at last," Nathan announced, returning with a steaming mug.

Sabrina accepted it. "Thanks." She managed a smile before taking a sip.

"While you're downing that, I'm going to bring my car around. It's a block away," he explained, smiling at Sabrina. "Meet me outside in about five minutes." He disappeared among the remaining party goers.

"I think it's awfully nice of Nathan to want to see you home," Kathy said. "You know we only discuss our displeasure over that interracial dating to each other. It's our silent frustration."

"Kathy, don't lecture me. I know I was wrong for letting the man know my feelings. He's already chided me and succeeded in making me feel guilty. Satisfied?"

"You're too much," Kathy said and laughed.

"I'd better get outside for my chauffeur." She reached in her purse for her car keys and handed them to Kathy. "Look out for my car. It's parked down the street. I'll get it sometime tomorrow."

"Sure thing," Kathy said, rising from the chair with her friend to assist her. She could see that Sabrina was still somewhat tipsy even though she had thrown up and had black coffee.

Taking a few steps, Sabrina wobbled on the fancy pumps she was wearing. She took hold of Kathy's arm as if she were a toddler learning to walk. As she teetered toward the front door, both of them giggled at her lack of grace.

"What could I have been thinking to wear these things tonight of all nights?" Sabrina asked. "You can see I'm not a rational woman."

"Well, they're kind of cute," Kathy said as they exited on to the porch. "Next time don't drink in them." She laughed softly. "There's Nathan pulling up in his car. His timing is perfect."

"What is left to say to him? I've said more than I should for the entire year." Sabrina grunted. "I'm not looking forward to being alone with him."

"Shut up and go on. He won't bite you, nor will he dump you on the side of the road like he should," Kathy teased.

Nathan's sleek black Maxima stopped in the middle of the street in front of Kathy's house. He hopped out of the car, which he left idling, and ran to the passenger side to open the door for Sabrina as she approached with Kathy.

"Make sure she gets in the house and is settled, Nathan. I'm holding you responsible for her," Kathy instructed as though she were Sabrina's mother.

"Don't worry. She's in good hands," Nathan assured Kathy, dashing to the driver's side.

"You live in that new subdivision, Tyler's Point, right?" Nathan asked Sabrina, settling in the car and then helping her fasten her seat belt.

Once Sabrina was comfortable, she became drowsy. "Yeah. 309...309 Clearfield Drive," she murmured and closed her eyes to ease the throbbing in her head.

As he drove, Nathan studied Sabrina's face. The streetlights illuminated her features, making her look vulnerable and sweet. If she would only give him a chance, he could show her how to enjoy life. And he was even capable of showing her what it was to be romanced by a man who really loved women. He glanced at her sleeping form. What Sabrina didn't realize was that he had more in common with her than she could imagine. He knew about loving and losing. He also knew how to survive. It was something he would be more than willing to share with her.

During the ride to her house, Nathan took a chance on disturbing Sabrina. He depended on the easy-listening jazz station on the car radio for company. He glanced at her sleeping form and felt sympathetic. Poor, sweet, tough Sabrina, he thought. Behind that hard, professional, successful exterior everyone saw each day, he suspected that there was a woman who only wanted to be pampered and loved by the right man. If she'd give him half a chance, he could be that man. But she had made it clear she wanted nothing to do with him socially. "Crossover Brother" was what she had called him. He should have felt offended and not even bothered to trouble himself with her. But he didn't hold grudges. He wasn't raised that way. And Sabrina posed a challenge to him. She aroused something in him that he had thought he wouldn't feel ever again.

As he parked in front of Sabrina's house, Nathan was hit by an idea that he was certain would teach her a lesson. Just something to make her think she wasn't faultless. By the time the sun came up, Sabrina wouldn't consider herself better than him. In fact, she would be the one wondering if she was still worthy of his respect. He went to her side of the car and was unable to awaken her completely. He rooted in her purse until he found her key ring. Then he scooped her in his arms and carried her to the house.

She sighed drowsily, hugged his neck and kissed his face, mumbling the name Malcolm.

Though he knew she longed for another man, he didn't mind one bit. One day her kisses and hugs would be for only him, he vowed.

Chapter Two

Sabrina had passed out from her overindulgence. Nathan undressed her with trembling fingers. He risked her ire and-worse yet-his reputation as an officer of the law. If she awakened, Sabrina could cause all kinds of trouble for him. With her business clout in the community, she could see to it that not only his career but also his involvement with the kids he loved would be ended. On the other hand, the devil in him led him to believe she deserved payback for the things she had said to him this evening and the way she had belittled his program at the Center.

He had her undressed. She lay limp on her bed, facing away from him. He removed her dress and was surprised to discover that she wore no bra. Sliding her bikini panties over her beginning to feel like a lecher instead of a prankster. He hadn't wanted to ogle the beauty of her flesh-her nudeness. Yet he couldn't resist the urge to admire her perfect, round breasts with their brown nipples looking like sweet gourmet chocolates. From her slender, graceful neck down to her pedicured feet, Sabrina had a body that was made to be adored and romanced. The heat of his lustful thoughts caused his member to grow long and heavy with desire. He ignored his response. To kill his urge, he contemplated her rude remarks from earlier in the evening.

Once he was satisfied with the way he had her positioned, he drew the covers over her to ward off the lascivious thoughts that he was struggling to restrain. As he tucked the comforter under her chin, she continued to sleep like a newborn babe.

All the liquor she had consumed had kicked in like a tranquil-izer, he reasoned.

Quietly moving around to the other side of the bed, Nathan proceeded to remove his own clothes down to his boxers. He tossed his sweater and jeans in the pile near the bed where he had scattered Sabrina's things. He removed two foil-wrapped condoms from his discarded wallet and opened them, then he pulled out a facial tissue from the box on the nightstand. He dipped the condoms into a glass of water and wrapped the unused condoms in the tissue, then dropped them into the wastebasket. He laid the wrappers on the nightstand beside the box of tissues.

Then he climbed into bed beside Sabrina. He considered snuggling close to her and touching her, but he didn't. It was too tempting. Instead, he turned away from Sabrina and flicked off the lights. Nestling beneath the covers, he decided that when he touched Sabrina it would be because she wanted him as much as he wanted her. He glanced toward the window and the cracks of the mini-blinds; the night was changing into the first morning of the new year. Being deceptive had worn him down. Listening to the sound of Sabrina's breathing, he grew drowsy. He hoped that she wouldn't end up hating him, he mused, giving in to the sleep that overcame him.

Sabrina opened her eyes to the morning light. She stretched and rolled on her back, then realized in horror she was naked and not alone in bed. Shocked by the situation, she blinked her eyes to clear them and to assess the bulk beside her. She tried weighing the events of the evening before-the party. Whom had she met to bring home to her bed? she wondered. Her blood ran cold, thinking that she had seduced some stranger and foolishly bedded him.

She placed her hand on her forehead and cursed herself for drowning her troubles in too much champagne. She knew she had a low tolerance for alcohol, but she had thrown caution to the wind and drank anyway. She raised up on her elbow to study the face of the masculine form beside her. Nathan Atkins! He lay on his back, sound asleep, with his arm covering his eyes. The tangled bedding they shared covered him from the waist down. He was bare-chested. Nude!

Sabrina bolted upright in bed and studied the fitted sheets that had come loose from the top of the mattress. What in the world had she done in her depressed and inebriated state? And with Nathan Atkins of all people! There was only one explanation for two people waking up in the same bed, butt naked, she reasoned. Sabrina grabbed her throbbing head.

Gazing around the room, she spotted a trail of her clothes mingled with his, leading up to the bed. She clutched her head and groaned loudly. "Oh my goodness," she uttered, as waves of shame washed over her.

Suddenly, she felt Nathan's moist, warm lips upon the back of her shoulder. She turned quickly, pulled the sheet over her breasts and shrank away from him.

He chuckled at her display of modesty. "Some night, huh?" His voice was husky from sleep and that morning-after sound of intimate satisfaction.

Swinging her feet to the floor, she stood and tugged the comforter from the bed to wrap around herself-to shield her nude body from his sight. "How did...did this happen?" Her brow creased with confusion. "My word! What could I have been thinking?" Her eyes rolled with self-loathing.

Brushing his hand over his hair, Nathan beamed with amusement. "Hmm...that you and I could be perfect? And you were certainly right about that." He grinned devilishly. "You're an exciting woman. Adventurous, too." He studied her with a lecherous smirk. "Don't look so troubled. Don't worry. I still respect you." His hazel eyes twinkled with mischief. He fell back upon the pillows and placed his hands behind his head, staring at her and beaming as if she had been a fantastic conquest.

Sabrina studied him, straining to remember what it had been like to surrender her body and self-respect to him. She

27

felt a surge of self-contempt.

Though she hid her body from Nathan, his steady gaze unnerved her. He raised himself up on his elbow, rubbed his chin and moistened his lips. The gleam in his eyes let her know that he remained titillated by their wanton actions between the sheets.

She imagined it gave him great pleasure to have scored with her. She did remember confronting him at the party about his interest in white women. Had she made some kind of crude offer to him to prove that black women were better lovers? Was that why she was in bed with him? She had done some crazy things while drinking; that was the reason why she usually had no more than one drink every now and then. Obviously he had accepted the challenge and brought her to her house to find out what it was like to be with a black woman-for old time's sake. With all these thoughts going through her mind, she didn't like herself. She had let down her guard and acted the way her partying mother would have. And though she loved her mother, Sabrina had worked so hard to break the negative reputation Grace Lewis had garnered over the years.

Nathan smiled wryly. "My goodness, Sabrina. There's nothing to be ashamed of. You and I are adults. We're only human. So what if we had our own little party? We just got caught up in the holiday."

She hated his glib remark. She stood ramrod straight. "I don't do one-night stands. You took advantage of me and the state that I was in. I accept my part in this debacle," she said in a querulous tone. "But it won't happen again! I can guarantee you that." She eyed him with cold determination. She wanted to smother that glint of passion, that gleam of victory in his eyes. Since her Malcolm ordeal, she had been resolved that neither Nathan-or any other man-would have a place in her life.

"Okay. Fine. I can live with that," Nathan said, sitting up in bed. "But I'll still have my memories. I'll always remember how wild and wonderful you were." He chuckled. "What happened here will be our secret." He patted the bed. "I'm not a kiss-and-tell kind of guy." He started to toss back the covers to get out of bed.

Sabrina threw up her hand to halt his actions. She didn't want to see his body. "Don't! Not until I'm out of the room," she demanded. Heat colored her face. What had happened during the night had been beyond her control, her reasoning. Alcohol and the emptiness of her heart had made her prime prey for Nathan. Her biggest mistake had been allowing him to drive her home. He must have had something like this on his mind all along, she thought. She did remember him being insistent on giving her a ride. She bet that all the while he was setting her up to be the object of his lust.

"Okay. Take it easy." He pulled the sheet over himself again.

She stiffened, momentarily abashed at her predicament. "I don't like asking for favors, but I'm really counting on you to keep this indiscretion between us. I'd die if anyone in Hunter's Creek learns that you and I have been...have..."

"Lovers?" Nathan arched his eyebrows at her, a grin tilting the corners of his mouth.

"No! Slept together. Love played no part in this ludicrous interlude." She sighed in exasperation. "I've worked too hard to earn a good name and respect in this town."

"Your reputation won't get tarnished," he vowed. "No one will ever know that you're an angel with a crack in her wings." He gave her a devilish grin. His eyes sparkled with delight.

She could no longer stand that smug look on his face. She made a quick, dramatic turn that caused her to get entangled in the comforter she used as a shield. The darn thing was still tucked tightly at the foot of her bed. The more she tugged, the more resistant the cover became. More of her body was revealed.

Nathan leaned toward the foot of the bed to free the darn comforter. She resisted his assistance, thinking he was trying to show off his nudeness.

She lifted her arms and waved him away. To her dismay,

the comforter fell away from her and exposed her completely. She gasped and folded her arms over her breasts. Seeing Nathan's gaze skimming her below the waist, Sabrina folded her knees together.

"Sabrina, you're too much." He laughed at her school-girl modesty.

Infuriated by his amusement, she turned, marched away from him and dashed into her walk-in closet. She drew the folding door shut behind her with a loud thud.

Hearing Nathan snickering at her mishap, she uttered an obscenity to herself. She reached up on the shelf for a pair of her sweatpants and a sweatshirt to cover her body. She wished her underwear was accessible to her. But she had too much pride to let Nathan see her rummaging through her dresser for a bra and a pair of panties. The sweats were loose-fitting enough to hide her full breasts, which jiggled a bit when she wore no support. What a mess, she thought, with a mixture of cynicism and humor. From the disheveled bed to the scattered clothes on the floor, Sabrina had sacrificed all of her dignity to that rascal, that traitor.

Dressed, she was more able to deal with Nathan. She snatched open the door to find him standing in black silky boxers. He greeted her with a broad smile and not an ounce of shame.

"I apologize for laughing," he said. "I meant no harm. Believe me, this is no catastrophe. There's no need for you to feel embarrassed. And I was careful." He stepped into his pants and yanked up his zipper. He reached over to the night-stand and showed her the condom wrappers, then he crumpled them and dropped them into the wastebasket.

Two! Two times! she thought, misery coursing through her. She wished she could vanish. She'd been nothing but a super freak. She was grateful he had had the sense to use protection, she thought with a flood of relief. She certainly didn't want any surprises like a STD or—heaven forbid—a pregnancy as a result of her thoughtlessness.

"Thank goodness," she said, holding her heart. "Look, I'm

going to the kitchen while you finish dressing. Both of us could use some coffee. It should be ready. I have one of those automatic coffeemakers." She padded barefoot out of the room before any more references to their intimacy could be made.

When Nathan appeared in the kitchen, Sabrina gave him a tight smile and offered him a steaming mug of coffee. At such an awkward moment, she had no idea what to say to him.

They sipped their coffee in silence.

"Uh...I've been going through a difficult time these last few months," she admitted softly. She wanted to explain her actions. She couldn't let him think she was an easy woman.

"I figured as much. The holidays have a way of making wounds worse. Believe me, I understand. You have no reason to feel ashamed for crying. I was glad I was here to hold you and to comfort you."

Sabrina's blood ran cold. Had she done that as well? My goodness, I made an utter fool of myself, she thought, staring into her mug.

"I know I should have resisted doing what I did," he went on. "Yet I was helpless when you looked up at me with those big, teary eyes of yours. I wanted to be your hero and to relieve you of the pain that was making you suffer. I held you and kissed you on the face like I would any dear, troubled female friend. But your response shook my restraint. You put your arms around my neck and kissed me sweetly. One thing led to another. I was so enchanted by you and all that you offered, I wasn't even bothered by the fact that you called me Malcolm." His eyes softened. "I wanted to be that man, who-ever he was, for one night," he said softly.

Hearing how loosely she had acted with Nathan, Sabrina was astounded. She didn't like what she heard. But she had to live with it.

Nathan set down his cup. "It didn't matter that you want-ed me to become someone else. I felt ten feet tall being want-ed by you. You were so easy to love." His eyes grew dreamy and his voice was so velvet smooth that she felt as though he was caressing her.

For a moment, Sabrina set aside her pride and allowed herself to be hypnotized by the wonderful look of admiration she saw in his eyes. She had to force herself to break his gaze. She knew that she had to be careful or she could end up making a whole new set of mistakes.

"I'm sorry for pulling you into my life-my problems," she said ruefully. "Believe me, I won't need that kind of comfort from you ever again. I'm strong. I'm used to looking out for myself." She turned away from him to hide her regret and walked to her kitchen window to assess the day.

Nathan eased up behind Sabrina. He placed his hands on her shoulders and kissed the top of her head. "What happened last night was part of our destiny. You might not like it. But it's done. Whether you like it or not, you and I have a bond that neither of us can ever deny or forget."

Sabrina closed her eyes and contemplated his words. She wanted nothing more than friendship from Nathan. She couldn't bear to think of a relationship with another man when she hadn't even gotten past the hurt, the humiliation with Malcolm. "I choose to forget it!" She held her head high. "It was only sex. Nothing more." She shrugged off his touch and moved away from him.

"Whatever," he said in a flat tone. He stared at Sabrina; her face had become a somber mask. "Happy New Year," he deadpanned. He grabbed his leather jacket and sauntered out the back door without looking back.

Sabrina went to the kitchen window to watch Nathan get into his car and pull away. Once he was out of sight, she couldn't understand why she felt guilty for the way she had slammed the door on any relationship. Why should she worry about hurting a "Crossover Brother" like him?

Sabrina sat in her kitchen, sipping tea and thinking over all her problems. What a way to begin a new year, she mused.

She shivered over all that had happened, then shrugged. It had happened and there was nothing she could do to go back to eradicate it. All she could do was to move forward and pretend what happened hadn't. It was the only way she knew to deal with it. How was she going to face Nathan? And could she really trust him not to brag about the details of their one-night stand?

To set aside the negative thoughts reeling in her mind, Sabrina decided on a long, leisurely bubble bath; it would help her forget the incident with Nathan and ease her frayed nerves. She had drawn her warm bath and added her scented bath salts, when she became aware of the doorbell ringing. She wanted to ignore it, but whoever it was was persistent. She scowled, wrapped herself in a pink terry cloth robe and marched off to the door. By the time she reached it, she heard her mother, Grace, calling her name as if she were down at the other end of the street.

"What took you so long, girl?" Grace asked. Instead of rushing into the house as she normally did, Sabrina's mother turned and shouted. "Come on, man! Hurry up!" she called to her companion who sat in a battered black pick-up truck. She turned back to Sabrina. "I don't want to bring you any bad luck coming across your door first on New Year's Day. It's got to be a man, to bring you luck. And I know there ain't no man been in this house since you lost your man."

"You and your superstitions," Sabrina said, shaking her head.

Dennis, her mother's current boyfriend, ambled up the walk to the house. "Hey there, Miss Sabrina," said the tall, dark-complexioned man. He wore a blue plaid flannel shirt and dusty looking jeans. "Happy New Year." He grinned at Sabrina, removing his cap before entering the house.

"The same to you," Sabrina said. "You can have a seat in the living room. The remote to the television is on the table."

"Thank you, ma'am." He lumbered off into the living room.

"Move out of my way, Dennis. I got to use the bathroom.

Been holding it in for the last hour." Grace hustled into the house, bearing covered plastic dishes. She shoved them at her daughter and rushed towards the bathroom. "Beer. It just rolls through me," she mumbled.

Sabrina met Dennis' gaze and smiled politely, then moved into the kitchen. She didn't like being left alone with him. She had only met Dennis one time, but she didn't care for him much. The shifty look in his eyes suggested that he was a man with a bad past. But then again, Sabrina never cared for any of the men who had been in and out of her mother's life. Grace's taste in men left a lot to be desired. Sabrina couldn't figure out why, as her mother got older, she didn't get any wiser about her men. This man, Dennis, worked as a short-order cook at the Soul Food Inn, where her mother had been working for the last fifteen years as a hostess/waitress.

"Phew! I feel a lot better," Grace announced, entering the kitchen with her coat across her arm. She tossed it on the back of a chair. Sabrina's mother wore a purple pantsuit that could have been a size larger to accommodate her hips. She had on a white sweater that fit snugly over her ample bosom. "I brought you some black-eyed peas and collard greens for luck and prosperity. I knew you wouldn't take the time to come see me and eat, or even take the time to cook them for yourself, so I brought the food to you. Be sure to eat them before the sun goes down." Grace dropped into a seat at the kitchen table, pulled out a cigarette and lit it with her plastic lighter.

"Thanks for the food, but I have no appetite for this stuff." Sabrina's stomach felt queasy as she looked at the black-eyed peas and collards in the clear containers. She wasn't quite over her hangover from the night before. "You shouldn't have gone through the trouble of coming all the way out here. I don't believe in those old folk tales anyway. Luck and prosperity come from hard work."

"I don't make this stuff up. I've heard it so long that I'm afraid not to follow the traditions. Who knows what could happen if we didn't do this stuff?" Grace chuckled. She took a drag off her cigarette and eyed her daughter intensely.

"You're going to start the year off grouchy, I see. Still haven't heard from Malcolm, huh?"

"I'm not grumpy. I told you that's over and done." Sabrina opened the fridge and placed the containers of food inside.

"Give me a beer while you're in there, baby."

"It's not noon yet, Mama. And you just had some, didn't you?"

"I want a beer," Grace said in a no-nonsense tone.

Sabrina reached in and got a can of beer and handed it to her mother with a judgmental look. The excesses of too many men, too many cigarettes, and too much liquor showed on her mother's almond-colored face, Sabrina thought. The good looks that her mother had been known for when she was younger had faded over the years. Her drop-dead figure was gone and she now had to shop in plus-size stores.

"Don't look at me like that, lady." Grace popped the top on the can of beer and took a long swallow. She made a face, then looked at the can. "Yuk! How can you drink this watered down stuff? This is like drinking a soda." She squinted at the can to see the words—lite beer. "Don't you have the real thing?" Though Grace complained, she continued to drink.

"It's all I've got," Sabrina snapped. "I don't drink it. My company drinks it."

"You never did answer my question about Malcolm. Don't tell me you're going to let some hussy take him from you." She finished off the beer and burped.

"No. I gave him to her. I'm through with Malcolm. I won't put up with him or any other man being unfaithful to me."

"You're so snooty. I can't believe you're my daughter. Sabrina, don't you know that if you want a man, you're going to have to share sometimes? Or at least put up some kind of fight to let the man know you care. Yep, all is fair in love and war. So, you caught him with another woman. Big deal." She shrugged. "You can't expect the man to go without a woman when he's living out of town. I don't ever want to have a man that no other woman wants." She let out a gutsy laugh.

Hearing this from her mother disgusted Sabrina. "I'm not like you. I don't ever intend to share a man. I'll do without companionship before I do something like that. I'm through with Malcolm. I don't want to talk about him." Irritated by her mother's lack of sympathy for her feelings, Sabrina walked to her window where she kept several potted green plants. She spotted one whose leaves had grown brown, and picked at the dried growth to hide her irritation.

Grace dragged on her cigarette and exhaled a puff of smoke. "You'd better make up with that man. He's going to be big-time-a superstar. He's a funny son-of-a-gun. Up there in New York, the door of opportunity will be opening soon. You'd better stick with him, so you can escort him through that door. Then you can have all the businesses you want, all 'cross the country, with the kind of money he'll be making."

Whirling around, Sabrina glared at her mother. "I don't need him. I don't want him. I'm doing all right by myself like I always have. I'll be what I want without anyone's help."

Grace puffed on her cigarette and gave her daughter a challenging look. "I may not have been the best mother in the world to you. But I did what I knew how. You always had food to eat and clothes to wear." Grace took one last puff off her cigarette and dropped it into her empty beer can. "I love you and you know it. I'm so proud of everything you've done. We've shown the people in Hunter's Creek that we can't be kept down, haven't we, baby?" Grace moved out of her chair and went to stand near Sabrina.

The whiff of her mother's strong, cheap perfume made Sabrina sick to her stomach because of her hangover. Grace gripped her child's shoulders. "Isn't that right, baby?"

"Yeah, sure." Sabrina was annoyed that her mother always wanted to take credit for her success. The only thing her mother had done was give her the motivation not to end up like her. Her mother had never had time for her and often placed her men before Sabrina's needs. She'd been blind to Sabrina's years of loneliness, her feelings of inadequacy. Grace's maternal instinct had only started to kick in when she saw the ambition Sabrina had. It seemed the more successful Sabrina became, the more maternal Grace wanted to be.

Grace tugged at her white sweater to cover her exposed bulging tummy. "Look, I'd like to stay longer. But Dennis and I are on our way to Jersey. Atlantic City. We want to spend the day playing the slot machines. I came by to get some cash. I'm running short."

"What happened to the money I gave you for Christmas?" Sabrina asked, thinking about the thousand dollars she had deposited in her mother's account.

"Well, I...Dennis has fallen on hard times. I helped him to get caught up with a few of his bills-get his truck fixed. He's going to pay me back. He promised."

The corner of Sabrina's mouth twisted in exasperation. She could never do enough for her mother. Growing up, she had tried to help her mother by cooking and cleaning the house. She had thought these actions would keep her mother home and not cause her to stay out late at night with men who never hung around long. She had thought by being a near-perfect child her mother would prefer to stay home with her so they could do the kinds of things she observed her friends' and classmates' mothers doing with them and for them.

Aggravated by the request for money but unable to deny it, Sabrina excused herself from her mother to get her purse. Even though she was a grown woman, she was still questing for the kind of mother love she'd fantasized about. Sabrina only had a few hundred dollars in cash on hand, but she was sure it wouldn't be refused.

"Thanks, baby." Grace took the money, folded it and stuffed it inside her bra. She leaned over and kissed her daughter. "You eat those goodies I brought you. I don't want you jinxed. I want you to have another good year."

Sabrina managed a weak smile. She wished she could confide in her mother the fact that her year was already off to a horrible beginning.

"Look, I'm leaving. Dennis and I want to get to Atlantic City before nightfall. I'll be back sometime tomorrow. I've got the evening shift at the Soul Food Inn," Grace babbled as she headed back to the living room where her man waited. "Come on, Dennis, sweetie. Let's hit the road!"

Dennis moved out of the chair and looked at Grace as if he wanted a signal that she had gotten money from her high-class daughter.

Grace pulled open the door for Dennis and told him she would be right out. She turned back to Sabrina. "I wish you would think about Malcolm. He's a good man. You know women are going to be throwing themselves at a fine-looking man like him. His heart is yours even though he might have strayed. No man is perfect."

Sabrina nibbled her bottom lip nervously to hold back her words. She didn't want to disrespect her mother—her only family.

Grace caressed her daughter's face. "You and I have to spend more time together, sugar. I haven't seen you since Christmas Day. Maybe when I get back, you and I can plan a mother-daughter day. Shopping, dinner and a movie. My treat, okay?"

"Sure. Give me a call," Sabrina said softly. She wanted to cry. She knew her mother had no intention of following through with such a plan. She was good for building up her daughter's hopes only to disappoint her. Sabrina had stopped clinging to her mother's promises long ago. Since she had moved out on her own when she was eighteen, she and Grace hardly took time to do anything more than chat on the phone. Grace went to Sabrina's salon, Raving Beauty, and got her hair done, free of charge because she felt it was one of her rightful privileges as Sabrina's mother. Whenever Grace showed up at the salon, anyone who saw the two of them together would have thought they had a close relationship. No one knew how much Sabrina resented her mother for acting like a teenager-an older sister instead of the mother she yearned for her to be. Grace always counted on Sabrina to make everything right for her instead of the other way around.

"Happy New Year, baby." Grace chuckled with cheer and

gave Sabrina a bear hug, suffocating her with the heavy scent of her perfume. Then Grace breezed out the door and hustled down the sidewalk to the curb where Dennis waited in his truck.

Sabrina's vision became blurry with tears. Watching her mother go off with her man, she felt like that little girl who was always left home alone because her mother chose to have a good time with her friends instead of spending time with her. "Happy New Year to me," Sabrina whispered to herself. Her heart ached with loneliness and regrets. What a way to start the year, she thought, closing the front door and locking it.

Chapter Three

Fifty-five-year-old Phyllis Graham's chestnut complexion grew more radiant with each layer of make-up that Sabrina carefully applied. The woman's demeanor also changed. She went from slumped shoulders to erect posture. As she admired her transformation, she held her head higher, and a self-assured gleam appeared in her eyes.

Mrs. Graham chuckled. "When Kathy, my oldest girl, gave me a gift certificate for your place, Romantic Poses, I thought it was a joke," she said to Sabrina. "I've been married for thirty-five years, reared five children and teach Sunday School, and I never miss a Sunday church service unless I'm sick. A place called Romantic Poses certainly wasn't the place for an older woman like me."

Using her make-up brushes to put the finishing touches on Mrs. Graham's face, Sabrina smiled. She went to work combing and styling the lady's wonderful black hair, which was streaked with gray. She made her look sophisticated and dignified.

Sabrina patted the older woman's hair to insure the shape of the hairdo she had given her. "A lot of my friends have the wrong impression of my business. They think it's all about sexy bedroom pictures, like younger women would take for their men. But it's more than that. Here is where I want women to come to make themselves feel glamorous in the way they feel comfortable. Beautiful. I bet you can't tell me the last time you had a decent picture of yourself made."

Mrs. Graham appraised herself in the mirror with a pleased

smile. "I can't tell you. After the kids started coming, I forgot all about myself and doing the kind of things to pamper myself the way I did when I was single."

"That's easy for a woman to do. Most women commit so much of their lives to their husbands and their children that they neglect the women they used to be." Sabrina was pleased with the transformation of Mrs. Graham. She also admired the wonderful wife and mother she had been. The woman was way overdue to have some fun and to start pampering herself. "Mrs. Graham, you might want to take a boudoir picture for your husband. Your kids are nearly grown. It's time to put the romance back..."

"Child, you want to get me in trouble? My husband might have a heart attack if he saw me all dolled up at my age like I was in one of those girly magazines." She laughed.

"You ought to think about it. I'll see to it that a tasteful job is done. You should pass the word of my place to your friends. I would love to have more older women come here. Just think how encouraging it will be to women like your daughter Kathy and me to know that as we grow older we can look better and more elegant. Just like you." She whirled Mrs. Graham around to the mirror so that she could have a full view of how great she looked.

"You've performed a miracle." Mrs. Graham smiled with pleasure.

"Now we have to get you dressed for your pictures. Go in the back to the dressing room and try on the things I've picked out for you. There are several nice outfits that should suit you perfectly."

"There's no lingerie, is there? I'm a grandmother."

"No ma'am. Not this time," she teased the woman. "I picked out outfits that you'll be comfortable in. And Camille Riley is a jewel of a photographer. She'll bring out your best features with her lighting and camera angles."

"I can see she is good." Mrs. Graham scrutinized the photos that hung around the Romantic Poses Salon. All of the portraits of the women, whether they were young or mature,

41

looked exquisite. "Did she take all of these pictures?"

"She sure did. And I intend to place your picture up there, too. You're going to be gorgeous and classy looking," Sabrina assured her, directing her toward the dressing room.

Once Mrs. Graham disappeared to dress for her pictures, Sabrina thought of the woman and her daughter. She envied the close relationship she had observed between Kathy Graham Mason, her good friend, and her mother. Phyllis Graham was the kind of mother that Sabrina wished her mother had been. Mrs. Graham acted like a mother should. She didn't walk around trying to look like she was younger than her daughter. She had managed to raise five kids and have a happy marriage for thirty-five years.

Sabrina figured that was the reason why Kathy had landed such a good, caring husband. She had had good examples in her life of what a man-woman relationship was all about by watching her loving parents. The only things that Sabrina had had to witness in her impressionable years were the disappointing relationships her mother had had through the years. She had seen men use and even abuse her mother on occasion. Yet her mother had grown no wiser. She kept making the same mistakes in the types of men she chose. All the wrong kind.

Sabrina feared that she was becoming like her mother with her choice of men. That helpless feeling of weary anxiety dropped over her. Hadn't she had her fair share of losers and users? And then she had chosen Malcolm to trust-to give love a try, one more time. For the last couple of years he had had her hoodwinked into thinking he really loved her. He had given her an engagement ring. Malcolm had filled her with hopes of a life that would be lived happily ever after with him. Believing that fairy tale had left a feeling of defeat buried in her heart.

And then, what had really frightened her was the encounter she'd had with Nathan Atkins on New Year's. It was something her mother, Grace, would do and wouldn't give a second thought to. Sabrina thought she had risen above the tasteless things she had seen her mother do. She didn't want to end up like her mother. A woman who had to define her self-worth by the presence of a man.

Sabrina peeked into the studio where Phyllis Graham was being photographed by Camille Riley. The older woman had chosen a lovely deep-rose dress. Her eyes twinkled with happiness and her good-natured personality. She had gone from being a plain, matronly housewife found shopping in the grocery store in one of those awful pantsuits with huge butterflies on the shirt, to a beautiful, classy woman. Kathy Mason and her family would be very pleased at how Romantic Poses had altered their mother.

While Mrs. Graham continued her photo session, Sabrina checked her appointment book. She glanced out the window and spotted Nathan Atkins across the street, approaching the Clip Joint, the barber shop. On this crisp winter day, he was dressed in a leather bomber jacket with a wool scarf wrapped around his neck. He wore aviator-style sunglasses to protect his eyes from the brightness of the cold day. He looked handsome and impressive; Sabrina's tummy quivered on the inside. She felt a mixture of shame and intrigue because of this man she'd known carnally but not personally. Before he entered the barber shop, he gave Sabrina's establishment a longing look.

It was the first time she had seen Nathan since that morning he had left her house two weeks ago. Sabrina had avoided Nathan. She couldn't bear to face him. She hadn't decided how she was going to manage a working relationship with him at the Hubbard Community Center after she had slept with him like an easy tramp.

Because of her shame, she'd neglected to do her volunteer work in the last couple of weeks at the Center. She hated disregarding the kids. But she was just too embarrassed to face Nathan. In time she would find the courage to return to the Center and to make up for her lost time. She didn't want to disappoint the girls whose confidence and respect she had worked so hard to gain.

At eleven o'clock that night, Sabrina stretched and yawned. She had worked late in the office of Romantic Poses, going over her schedule and the wardrobe her clients had requested for the rest of the week. Exhausted from a long and extremely busy day, she decided it was time for her to hire an assistant. She and Camille, her photographer, had managed to get the business thriving. So much so that Sabrina could afford to pay for extra help now

There was no doubt in her mind that by the time she took a hot shower she would fall fast asleep from her good hard work. Tonight she wouldn't toss and turn and worry over all the mistakes and the sorrow she tried not to think about.

Exiting Romantic Poses, located in the new South Point Shopping Center, Sabrina dashed for her car, which was parked two doors away from her business on the now nearly-empty parking lot. She reached her car and hit the button of the alarm system on her key ring to unlock the doors. As she took hold of the handle of the car door, she was suddenly seized from behind. She gasped in fear, feeling the strong arms slide around her waist.

"Hmm...you feel so good, lady. A body like yours is too much for any man to ignore." A male body pressed into hers. "You need a bodyguard like me to cover you." The man spoke into her ear, holding her flush to his body.

Registering the sound of the voice, Sabrina found her panic turning to anger. She stomped the man's foot as hard as she could.

The man cursed and yowled with pain, releasing her. "Dag it, woman! I was only playing, baby." He winced from his injured foot.

"Malcolm, have you lost your mind? You nearly gave me a heart attack." She placed her hand over her heart and exhaled deeply to ease the pounding. "Why aren't you in New York with...with that hussy?" Feeling more in control, she placed a hand on her hip; she was all set to give him a piece of her mind.

The nearby streetlight illuminated Malcolm Knight's face.

Despite her anger and his frightening antic, Sabrina's couldn't restrain her physical attraction to him. Though in her mind she had decided that their romance was over, her body still responded with a tinge of sexual desire for him. But she determined not to get entangled in Malcolm's lies or that enticing look in his eyes that often weakened her in the past.

"I had to see you. I drove all the way from New York, hoping I could talk to you, reason with you to set things straight between us," he said. "You're still a workaholic, I see. I thought I'd never see you leave. I felt like a stalker, sitting like a stalker, sitting outside your place waiting for you to appear," he said with humor to charm her. "Knowing how pissed you were with me, I had to slip up on you or else you wouldn't have let me near you." He stood and grinned that boyish grin with that small gap between his front teeth. His brown face, his high cheekbones, his almond-shaped eyes could easily have given him a career as a male model instead of the comedian dream he'd chosen to follow. "You almost crippled me," he said. "I hate to think of what you would have done had you known I was out here, waiting on you." He leaned on her car and held out his hand for hers. "Don't be so cruel, 'Brina. We can work our problems out."

She folded her arms at her waist. "I don't want to work anything out! I'm tired of being your joke, Malcolm. It's over!" She waved him out of her way to dismiss him so that she could get to her car.

Malcolm didn't budge an inch. "Won't you give a brother a chance? Stop being stubborn. Will you listen to me? You have to hear me out, precious," he implored. "We've got too much history together to end the good thing we had."

"Shut up, Malcolm! I want to forget our ridiculous history. I've had my fill of your half-truths, your promises, and the way you've pretended to love me. Admit it! You kept me hanging on because I was your sponsor. Now that I've had my wake-up call, you're going to have to get off your butt and get a real job to pay your way. Or maybe your slumber partner, that sex kitten, will help support you," she snapped.

"You don't have to go there, Sabrina. Yes, you were helping me out, but I promised to pay you back every dime. And I mean it! That was the deal when I left Hunter's Creek."

"And I'm suppose to believe that after you promised to love me, too? You convinced me you meant that until I caught you playing house." She grew angrier the more she thought of the emotional wringer he had put her through. She let out a groan of disgust and stepped up to him, attempting to nudge him out of the way with her body. "Get out of my way!" She pounded on his shoulder. "I'm tired of wasting words with you. You make me sick on my stomach!"

"Hold on!" Malcolm placed his hands on her arms to control the blows she threw at him. "I'm sorry. I was a dog. Just give me another chance and I'll prove to you that you're the only woman I'll ever need. That woman is out of my life. She's gone for good, 'Brina."

"But she's still in my mind." She touched her forehead. "Every time I close my eyes, I still see you and her, tumbling in your bed that evening I came to surprise you in New York." She grew breathless from her fury. "That's one act I refuse to follow. There's no way I can let you touch me after what I've seen." Angry tears spilled from her eyes. "Let me go! Stay away from me!" She pushed at him and wiggled free.

As she stormed away to compose her chaotic emotions, Malcolm went after her. He snagged her wrists and held them tightly. "I'm miserable. I'm going down without you, baby. I can't be creative. I've bombed in the last few gigs I had. You're my good luck charm. I have to have you back in my life." He scooped his arms around her and pressed his warm lips over her cold ones. One of his hands slid down to her bottom and he pulled her against his growing arousal.

Sabrina's temper flared at his insolence. She knew Malcolm had probably assumed that all it took to ease the tension from their differences was his special, tender loving to set things right with her. She allowed her body to grow pliant in his arms. She pretended that all was well until she could think of a way to be rid of him without a hassle.

Malcolm was clearly encouraged and believed that he had put one over on her-again. It was with this confidence that he parted her lips with his forceful tongue to stir her even more. He closed his eyes to savor her surrender; she bit his tongue. He jumped away from her, sputtering with sounds of pain.

She glared at him with burning, reproachful eyes. "I meant what I said. I'm not falling for your charms anymore, Malcolm. As far as I'm concerned, you can step in front of a speeding car." She backed away from him. Misery assailed her, thinking how this man had taken advantage of her love and kindness one too many times.

Giving her a determined look, Malcolm came after her. He seized her again, entrapping her in a tight embrace. "I won't give up on us. I can't believe you mean the things you said. If you didn't care, you wouldn't be so furious with me," he said in a sexy tone. He gripped the back of her neck and rested his forehead against her forehead.

"I...I can't do this anymore," Sabrina cried, straining away from his determined hold. "Turn me loose," she pleaded. "I refuse to give you another chance to hurt me."

"I won't hurt you," he said emphatically. "I promise, 'Brina." He held onto her. He forced kisses upon her in an attempt to quell her and to win her back.

"No! I don't want you. Get away!" she sputtered against his forceful mouth. She managed to wrestle out of his embrace but not completely away from the grip he held on one of her arms.

"Be quiet, 'Brina. Stop acting as though I'm trying to hurt you. Let's go to your place where we can talk this thing out to some kind of agreeable resolution."

Despite the fact she battled him, he held her by her wrists and yanked her back to him.

Just then, a police car with flashing blue and red lights zoomed up to them on the parking lot. Two officers emerged from the car and rushed toward Sabrina and Malcolm.

"All right, buddy, step away from the lady," the officer ordered in a no-nonsense tone.

47

Sabrina's head snapped around to the sound of Nathan's voice. Though she was relieved at their assistance, she also deplored his presence. He of all people had to be the one to come to her rescue, she thought, feeling embarrassed.

"Okay, Sabrina. Talk to me. What's the deal here?" Nathan walked up to Malcolm and ordered him to assume the position for a search. "Pat this character down," he snarled to his partner.

"Officer, everything is cool. Really it is," Malcolm babbled nervously before Sabrina could utter a word. "My lady and I were just having a difference of opinion."

Nathan stood akimbo with his hand on his holster. Observing Malcolm and then Sabrina, he exuded authority with the somber appearance of one who expected instant obedience. "From what I could see, it looked as though this man was trying to harm you," Nathan said in a cool, professional tone.

Sabrina sniffled and brushed tears from her eyes.

"What's happening? Talk to me. Is what this character said the truth?" Nathan asked.

"Atkins, he's clean," announced his partner.

"Check his I.D., Roberts," Nathan barked. "It's your call, Sabrina. You want to file charges for assault, harassment, I can run him in."

Sabrina hesitated and studied Malcolm. He gave her a pleading look. She considered having him booked to even the score for the way he had humiliated her, used her. She expelled a sigh of resignation. "That won't be necessary. Really. I only want to get home. And I want him to stay away from me." She shot a no-nonsense look in Malcolm's direction.

The officer named Roberts took the I.D. Malcolm handed him and shined his flashlight on it. "This is a Malcolm Knight, age thirty. According to this, he is a resident of Hunter's Creek."

Sabrina felt a warm flush of shame on the back of her neck. She knew that Nathan now had the satisfaction of confronting the man who had broken her heart. She studied Nathan's face, and didn't see any triumph or mockery there. Feeling gratitude at the sincerity she sensed in Nathan, she realized that he wasn't going to embarrass her further about the man whom she considered a part of her past.

"All right, Mr. Knight. You heard the lady. No more trouble. Understand?" Nathan said. "Next time we might not be as cordial."

Roberts returned the wallet to a sullen Malcolm. "Okay, buddy. Let's go. Let's move it!"

Malcolm eyed Sabrina. His expression showed that he couldn't believe that she had considered having him locked up.

Sabrina wouldn't return her ex-lover's scrutiny. She wanted him to vaporize and for this awkward moment to end.

"I wasn't going to harm her, sir. I'm not like that and she knows it," Malcolm replied, eyeing Sabrina contemptuously as he sauntered away toward his car, which was parked on the street.

"Would you like for us to follow you home?" Nathan asked Sabrina in a soothing voice as he watched Malcolm get into his car, pull into traffic and vanish. Then he gave Sabrina a warm look.

"No, I'll be fine now. Thanks for your assistance." She attempted to smile and sound relaxed, getting into her car.

"Just doing my job," Nathan said. "Fasten that seat belt, okay? Are all your doors locked?" He peeked in to inspect them. "I'm not leaving until I see you off. And a word to the wise. Try not to be out this hour of night alone. There have been several crimes reported in this area. Until the suspect or suspects are arrested, you need to be extra careful."

Her mind fluttered with anxiety at his revelation of crime and the ordeal she'd been through with Malcolm. "Yeah...yes, officer," Sabrina said, respecting Nathan's advice as a law official. She locked her car door and fastened her seat belt. She turned on the ignition and hit the button to ease her window down. "Thanks again. Good-night, Officer Atkins," she said in an appreciative tone.

Nathan glanced over his shoulder; his partner was seated behind the wheel of their patrol car. He leaned down to Sabrina. "Can I call you later to talk? Uh...there are some things concerning the Center I'd like to discuss with you." His professional facade faded. He gazed at her as an intrigued man and not a police officer on duty.

The beginning of a smile tipped the corners of her mouth. What a thoughtful way to end the awkwardness and the tension that had existed between them since the New Year's ordeal, she thought. He was far more a gentleman than Malcolm had ever been. "Sure. Do that. I need to be caught up on what's happening there. I've been away from the kids too long. Well...good-night," she said in a friendlier tone. She eased the car into drive and pulled away from him toward the exit of the parking lot.

Checking her rearview mirror, she saw Nathan, standing tall and proud, still observing her. His interest flattered her. She knew it went beyond his duty. She was touched by his genuine concern. She decided that it was time for her to stop treating him as though he had been the only one to blame for the one-night stand. It was time for her to rid herself of that anti-male chip she'd carried on her shoulder and to accept the friendship that Nathan was clearly willing to share with her.

Chapter Four

"Hey, College Boy! Looking good, my man," Nathan enthused, greeting his younger brother, Randall. He had shown up at the Hubbard Community Center on this biting cold Saturday afternoon in February to visit and have his brother go shopping with him. Nathan got up from his desk where he had just gotten off the telephone, making arrangements for a field trip.

"You don't look so bad yourself, big bro'." They embraced and smiled with admiration at one another. Their broad smiles revealed their mutual resemblance. The same eyes that crinkled with mirth and open, friendly faces that mirrored the features of their late father.

"How are things at the university?" Nathan asked, taking a seat on the edge of the desk. "Graduating with honors, right?"

"You know it. I'm hanging in there. It's what dad would have expected. Can't wait for graduation in a few months." Randall grinned.

"Are you ready for the real world, man?"

"The question should be-Is the real world ready for me?" Randall dropped his lean, tall body into the folding chair in front of Nathan's desk.

"You're full of it." Nathan laughed. "Pops would be so proud of you, man." Nathan studied his twenty-one-year-old brother, who had grown into a fine young man. It seemed like only yesterday he was tagging behind him, getting on his nerves, being a pest, trying to hang out with him and his friends.

"I'm glad you agreed to go shopping with me for my lady friend for a Valentine's gift. You're the man when it comes to charming the ladies. And this is one lady that I want to win badly." Randall's brown eyes lighted with tenderness at the mention of his latest infatuation.

"I don't know how much help I can be in the romance department. I'm sort of out of touch with what the ladies want these days. But I'll be more than happy to go with you to see what we can come up with. Who is this lady who has you digging deep in your pockets without whining about a price for a gift?"

Randall's eyes twinkled. "Ariana Hendricks," he said softly. "Man, she is gorgeous and smart and sexy."

"Hmm...quite a lethal combination."

"She could be the one, Nate. Whenever she is near me, she makes my heart feel like it's going to burst. It scares me, the way I feel. I've never felt this way before."

Nathan laughed. "That's all right." He nodded his approval. "I hope you have the same outstanding effect on her. Or else you're in big trouble," he teased. "It's time you met someone nice, you rascal."

"She feels the same way, too. I think. I haven't given her reason to feel any other way, man. We've been seeing each other for a while. Of course neither of us has said the L-word yet. But I intend to come clean on Valentine's Day. That's why I need you to help me pick out something that's going to make me special in her heart."

"No material thing can do that," Nathan advised. "But it's a good idea to give her something to remind her of your love. You're putting a lot of pressure on me. I feel like I'll be the one to blame if you can't win this woman over with this gift you're going after." Nathan chuckled.

"Don't make fun of me, man. You know how it is when a man loves a woman. You've been there, so don't pretend you don't."

Nathan's brow furrowed deeply. "Oh yeah, I've been there a couple of times. This romance business is a risky one and it can be expensive."

"Expensive?" Randall's eyebrows lifted with concern.

"Not financially, but emotionally. When you love some-one, you lay your heart, your pride on the line. And you can get both of them stomped on by that woman you thought was going to be your angel for life." Nathan grew pensive. He thought of the price he had paid for falling for the wrong woman. After that experience, he had gone into emotional shock. For a while, he had refused to allow himself to feel. It had only been recently that he realized that he was healing. There was one woman, Sabrina Lewis, who made him feel alive, revitalized.

In the last few weeks, Sabrina had been much friendlier to him. But her warmth made him feel guilty. He didn't feel worthy of her kindness. He still hadn't broken down and told her the truth concerning what really happened New Year's. Every time she smiled at him or exchanged a friendly word, he felt like such a heel. He knew he should have been straight-forward with her by now. But he had been a coward. He did-n't want to risk losing her trust or the friendship that had devel-oped between them. Neither of them had mentioned the indis-cretion that had occurred after that party at the beginning of the year. When they were at the Center, Somebody's working with the kids, they were cordial toward each other. Sabrina appeared to be more comfortable with him. He was looking forward to chaperoning this Valentine's Dance that Sabrina had cooked up-more than the teenagers. In fact he looked for-ward to the dance just to be with her. He intended to ask her out on Valentine's, hoping she would be in a cheerful mood. The thought of having an opportunity to spend some time with Sabrina caused him to decide to hold out a little longer with his confession.

Suddenly, Sabrina appeared at the door. Nathan felt a surge of elation. "Nathan, I've been looking for you." She glanced at Randall and smiled. "Oh, excuse me. I didn't know you had someone visiting you."

"It's okay. Sabrina, this is my baby brother, Randall.

Randall, Sabrina Lewis. She's one of the volunteers here."

Sabrina was a delight for sore eyes. She wore a lime green sweater and black jeans that showed off her sexy, curvy, yet petite form. Her shiny raven hair was worn loose and wavy; it framed her delicate, flawless face, making her look like a college student.

Randall's eyes lighted with approval. He tugged shyly at his collar and mumbled a hello.

Sabrina leaned casually against the wall. "Nathan, don't forget you're supposed to help me decorate the gym for the Valentine's Dance. I've brought in all the decorations. I stored them in the supply room."

Nathan made a mock sigh. Yet he was secretly glad that she needed him. "I did promise to help, didn't I?"

"And get some of your young men to help, too. I intend to deodorize and transform that smelly gym into a fantasy land fit for Cupid. Scented candles and flowers will be everywhere," she said. "Remember, the dance is next Saturday evening from seven to eleven. I want you here no later than five o'clock to finish off any incidentals."

"Yes, boss," he said. He met her gaze and smiled warmly at her.

"You're too much." She shook her head and mimicked his kindly expression. "I've got to go. Nice meeting you, Randall." She whirled away and sashayed out of the office.

"Now that's a fine woman!" Randall gushed. "Are you down with her?"

"No, I am not down...seeing her socially." Randall hesitated at the use of his brother's crude slang in terms of Sabrina.

"She has a man?" Randall gave his brother a questioning look.

Nathan shrugged. Since that night he had encountered Sabrina with Malcolm, she had been more cordial to him. They'd talked several times. But their conversations dealt only with activities and the kids who came to the center. "Listen, I don't delve into her personal life. We work here together. Nothing more."

"If I were you, I would sure be trying to get next to her. She is sweet," Randall enthused. "She's perfect for you. You ought to make that move, bro'."

"Let me handle my social life. Right now, you handle Ariana." His eyes crinkled mirthfully at his brother's suggestion.

Randall laughed. "What time can we leave to shop? I want to get back to campus by eight. I have a date with Ariana and I don't want to be late. I hope we find something today. I won't be able to shop any other time."

"Chill out, Randall. I'll be ready to leave in a little bit. Let me clear away this stuff." Nathan proceeded to stack papers and stuff them in the file cabinet beside the desk.

"Mom told me to remind you to call her. She said she hasn't heard from you in a couple of days."

"She worries too much," Nathan said, pausing to rub his chin pensively. "I've been meaning to call her. It's just that Mom grills me so bad. She fears that I'm hiding some kind of emotional trauma from her and not getting on with my life." He shook his head.

"She wouldn't worry so badly if she knew you had a lady in your life. She would be thrilled if you brought someone like Sabrina to visit." He gave his brother a knowing grin. "Mom hates the idea that her favorite son might be lonely and loveless in Hunter's Creek." Randall placed his hand over his heart and gave his brother a twisted smile.

"Mom is too much, isn't she? She watches too many soap operas. She can turn everything into a drama if you let her." Nathan closed the file drawer. Then he straddled a nearby chair. "I'll make a point of calling her tonight. I'll give her a chance to fill me in on all the neighborhood and family gossip. Oh, I have to order flowers for her for Valentine's as well. I won't be able to get home that day."

"You sure know how to make her happy." Randall laughed. "That woman loves to talk to anyone who will listen."

Suddenly aware of shouts of obscenities and arguing outside the Center, Nathan bolted from his chair to the window to see what the commotion was. Two teen boys faced off, all set to go into battle. Their faces twisted in anger, they shoved each other and made threats of violence.

Nathan lifted the window. "Hey, I'm not going to have that junk around here. Play ball or else take your behinds home!" His voice rumbled with annoyance.

Both boys shot Nathan a defiant glance.

"I mean what I say! Don't make me come out there and clear the court!"

The boys' defiance crumbled under Nathan's stern authority.

"It's cool, Mr. Nate," said one of the boys. "Shoot the ball, man," he ordered to the one he had been ready to fight.

The ball was set into play between the boys once again. Nathan slammed the window shut.

"I would take my ball and go home," Randall teased. "You sure didn't cut them any slack."

"I can't afford to let them get away with anything. They have to know I mean business or else they'll run over me and disrespect everyone who comes here. That's what I'm here for. I'm trying to teach them how to respect and compromise without turning every issue into a war, a gun battle. Most of these boys aren't fortunate to have a father, like we did, to teach them things like we learned at an early age."

Randall nodded in agreement. "I sure miss Pop. I think about him all the time," he said softly.

"So do I. He was quite a man in more ways than one."

"Come on, man, you can't be serious about this woman if you're choosing that stinking cologne," Nathan teased his brother, Randall.

"It's not that bad. And besides, it fits my budget." Randall sniffed the cologne at the cosmetic counter.

"I thought you wanted to impress this woman." Nathan walked around the counter and found a fragrance that had a delicate scent. "This is what you need. This matches that young lady's personality, from what you've been telling me."

Randall took a whiff and grinned. "Yeah, this is her. I'd love to smell this on her." He peeked at the price. "Oh heck, I can't afford that!"

"Don't worry. I'll take care of it. My treat." Nathan reached into his pocket for his wallet and handed the woman a fifty-dollar bill. "It's good to know that someone is getting lucky in love."

"Gee thanks, Nate. I was hoping that big-brother caring would kick in."

"You set me up. You little runt." Nathan slapped him on the back. "Use your money for flowers. Roses would be ideal." The moment he mentioned the gift of flowers, Sabrina came into his mind.

Randall rubbed his chin thoughtfully. "Hmm...flowers would be a great touch. She'll think I'm one classy dude, huh? Hey, just call me Casanova." Randall's face brightened over his romantic gestures. With all of Nathan's advice, he seemed certain that he was going to make a love connection with Ariana.

"One more suggestion, little brother. Don't send the flowers. You take them to her. That look on her face will be something you'll never forget. It will change your life forever."

"Now that's some deep stuff. But I'm ready to deal with it if it means winning her affection." Randall looked at his brother with open admiration for all the lessons he was giving him. "You're the man!" He threw up his hand to accept a high five from his brother.

"I don't know about that. If I had all the answers, I wouldn't be alone. And I would know where Amber was." This subject always troubled him, made him feel sad.

"Caroline will turn up with Amber. She'll come to her senses and know what she's doing isn't right." Randall touched his brother on the shoulder to show he was feeling his frustration.

"I keep praying that will happen. But you know how vindictive that woman turned out to be when I got a divorce. And I fear she isn't capable of dealing with Amber properly."

"It's awful the way she's treated you. I don't see how you've managed to deal with what she's done."

"Right now, I have no other choice but to hang on. I 'm concerned about Amber. I don't want to waste energy on getting revenge or on petty games that Caroline wants to play," Nathan said somberly.

"If you need me, I'm only a phone call away," Randall said uneasily. He knew this subject was still a sore point for his older brother. Come on and let's get something to eat. I'm starving."

Nathan forced a smile. "You're always starving. Let's get out of this mall and to some place where we can get a man-sized meal and some beer."

Strolling out of the mall, Nathan listened half-heartedly to his brother blabbering about sports scores, astronomical salaries and injuries of superstar athletes. Nathan was too busy thinking about Amber. A sense of melancholy consumed him. It took everything in him to hide the emotion from his younger brother, who was so full of hope and excitement over the love he was ready to declare.

Nathan sat across from Sabrina at one of the cluttered tables where the kids had eaten a tasty buffet supplied by her generosity. He felt a sudden tension within him. Now that the dance was over and the kids had left, it was time for him to learn whether she would accept a date. "How naive was I to think that being a chaperone would only require me to stand on the sides and watch?"

Sabrina was pleased with herself for the positive outcome of the dance. Her wariness toward Nathan had subsided. She and he had been quite a team for the function. "And how insane was I to think that getting these teenagers to dress up would keep them from doing all that wild, suggestive gyrating like on those provocative music videos? Who'd have thought those girls could 'work it' a little too seductively in high-heels? You saw how all that rap music fired them up. All some of them needed was a bed if we had given them the chance to get away with it." Sabrina shook her head, chuckling. "It was good that you and I were here to remind them of the proper behavior expected of young ladies and young men."

"But some of them managed to find a few darkened corners for stolen kisses and embraces. We couldn't be everywhere at once."

"Next year, we'll recruit more adults to chaperone. I'm determined to show these kids they don't have to be tasteless to have a good time." Relaxing, Sabrina leaned on the table. "It was nice of you to give the guys that single rose to give to each girl who came. Did you see the look on the girls' faces when they received that flower? I'm sure that's something they're going to hang onto for a long time. It's obvious that for one night they were made to feel special."

"That was my intention. I've been working with my guys. I've been talking to them about how to treat a woman like a lady, not just look at her as a sex object. I think some of what I've been saying is getting through to them. Haven't you noticed the way the guys are holding open doors and not using profanity around here?"

Sabrina smiled at Nathan. She was impressed by his positive influence. He had definitely changed the attitudes of quite a few of the older guys. Sabrina had seen him talking with them. And she could tell by the way they looked at Nathan they admired him and wanted to be the cool, classy man that he was.

"Excuse me. I have a surprise for you. I can't let my guys outdo me." Nathan rose from his seat and hurried to the kitchen.

Sabrina stood and stretched. She had worn a tailored white suit and a red satin blouse and red satin pumps. During the dinner and dance, she had caught Nathan studying her with a soft look that reminded her of that one evening they'd shared.

The evening she had tried to block out of her mind. The behavior was totally out of character for her. Yet she clearly had been driven to that behavior because of depression, heartache.

Nathan reappeared from the kitchen with a glint in his eyes. One arm was hidden behind his back.

"What are you up to, Atkins?" Sabrina asked. He reminded her of the teen boys when they tried to approach the girls but were too shy to do it with confidence.

"These are for you," Nathan said. From behind his back, he whipped out a bouquet of cellophane-wrapped yellow roses with sprigs of baby's breath. He handed the bouquet to her and bowed slightly in a courtly manner.

At the sight of the beautiful, full roses, Sabrina felt a rush of joy that exhilarated her. "Oh Nathan, they're beautiful." Her eyes danced with delight as she studied them and smelled their wonderful fragrance. No one had ever given her flowers. Her mind flashed back to the last few years she'd been with Malcolm. She thought of the cheesy lingerie he'd bought her to model in front of him before they made love. Though she pretended to like his gift, she would much rather have had something that was tasteful that she could have shown off with pride.

"But you shouldn't have," she said to Nathan, feeling like an innocent girl. She sniffed the aromatic bouquet; she touched the petals, smiling and thinking he had been much too generous after the way she had treated him, the cruel things she had said at the party and the morning after.

Nathan knew he would never forget how her ebony eyes glistened with joy from his surprise. The beautiful look was indeed priceless. He hoped that Randall had received the same bit of pleasure for his deed. "I wanted to. You've worked so diligently with the kids. I wanted to make you feel special on Valentine's, too." He gazed at her, admiring the radiance of her face as she clutched the flowers.

Sabrina was clearly touched. She stepped up to Nathan and stood on tip-toe to place a kiss upon his cheek.

Nathan fought against the urge to sweep her into his arms to kiss her deeply and passionately. Instead, he steeled himself and smiled dreamily in appreciation. "Listen. It's been a long night for us. How about letting me take you to Jazzville? It's a cozy spot where we can unwind, have a few drinks..."

Cradling her flowers, Sabrina shot him a cautious look. "Drinks?" she asked uneasily.

"Uh...you can have a soft drink or coffee or tea," he said quickly. He laughed. "Believe me, I only want to share your company. I don't want to be alone tonight. The least we can do is finish our evening with some conversation and some sounds."

Sabrina liked his suggestion. Because she had been busy most of the day, she hadn't had a chance to wallow in self-pity as she had done with the previous holidays. And she was beginning to come to terms with her disappointment and her failed relationship with Malcolm. Once she had accepted her responsibility in the thoughtless liaison she had shared with Nathan, she began to see that he was really a nice man. And she had been grateful to him for not disclosing details to anyone or even mentioning it to her.

"Sure. That sounds wonderful," she enthused.

Nathan's extraordinary hazel eyes glowed with excitement and he flashed her an endearing smile. "Let's get out of here." He offered her his arm.

She slid her arm through his while still cradling her Valentine bouquet. Her heart was light and her spirits soared for the first time in months.

The moment that Sabrina and Nathan breezed into the club, Jazzville, they were washed in the sultry harmony of a trio. The singers backed a lovely woman who moaned sensual lyrics to a classic jazz ballad. The place was crowded with couples, sitting cozily and regarding each other with open fondness on this holiday of romance.

The hostess found a table for Sabrina and Nathan in the middle of the club. Seeing all the lovers around her, Sabrina felt a twinge of loneliness. But that was soon forgotten when she looked into Nathan's warm face.

"This is nice, isn't it?" He smiled at her and signaled for a waitress.

"Hmm...it sure is," Sabrina agreed, feeling buoyant. She reveled in his open admiration for her. The waitress appeared.

Nathan touched her hand. "Sabrina, what would you like?"

Sabrina glanced up at the waitress. Beyond the woman, she caught a glimpse of Malcolm. He sat at the bar, hunched over a drink. A sudden spurt of adrenaline shot through Sabrina's veins. He was the last person she wanted to see. She was irked by his presence. Was it a coincidence for him to be here? Or had he followed them? She dreaded the thought of another irrational confrontation with him. "Uh...I'll take a cola, please," she told the waitress in a cheery tone to mask her concern from Nathan.

Hopefully, Malcolm wouldn't even see her and be on his way. She wanted a glass of wine to calm the arrival of anxiety. But she dared not risk a drop of alcohol after her last experience on New Year's. She had decided to do her drinking in the privacy of her home when she was alone and wouldn't have any embarrassing consequences to deal with.

"I'll have scotch on the rocks," Nathan told the waitress. He turned in his seat and looked toward the stage where the woman worked her song as though she were rendering a piece of her own life. "She's too much, isn't she?" He bobbed his head in time to the rhythm.

Sabrina heard the music, but she wasn't into the groove. She was too busy wondering what Malcolm would do if he realized she was there. She toyed with her gold bracelet, wishing he would leave so that she could enjoy her evening with Nathan.

Suddenly, Nathan sat upright in his chair with a flash of recognition and grinned broadly. "There's a friend of mine from college," he said, rising from his seat. "Excuse me. I have to go say hi and see what he's up to. I'll be back in a minute."

Left alone at the table, Sabrina felt self-conscious. She had just about decided to go to the ladies' room to touch up her make-up and avoid the possibility of Malcolm singling her out.

"Sweetness, what a pleasure to see you here." Malcolm touched Sabrina's shoulder and then plopped into Nathan's seat.

Sabrina's face hardened. "What are you doing here? I thought you had returned to New York."

"I did. But I drove back to visit my mom, to see you again." He smiled.

"You must leave me alone." She gave him a dark, smoldering look. "I'm with someone. I won't have you ruining my evening. You're going to have to leave," Sabrina said calmly though her heart raced with anger.

Ignoring her words, Malcolm slid his chair closer to her. "You look wonderful." He attempted to take her hand, but she recoiled from him.

"Malcolm, I don't want any trouble. I came here to relax, to have fun. Do me a favor and leave," she said in a controlled voice. She settled back in her chair, folded her arms and crossed her legs, glaring at him.

Raising one eyebrow in a questioning slant, he gazed at her. "You're trying to replace me, huh? You know you can't do that. I meant too much to you, baby." He gave her a defiant smile. "You belong to me. I know what it takes to please you. 'Brina, you like what I do for you too much." He chuckled, then moaned softly. "I get hot thinking about that sweet sound of surrender you have when..." He reached over and caressed her knee.

Sabrina uncrossed her legs and shifted them to avoid his touch. "Shut up! And get out of my face, Malcolm. Why don't you go back to the Big Apple and stake your claim on all that fame you've sold your soul for?"

"I can't leave Hunter's Creek until I've squared things with you, baby. I'll keep returning when I can so you and I can settle our differences and get back to our lives and the way it used to be between us." He leaned toward her. "You've punished me enough. The rules are clear to me. You're in control. Isn't that what turns you on anyway? Calling all the shots in a relationship."

Sabrina was glad when she saw Nathan returning to their table. The sight of him eased her anxiety about this man who stirred a gamut of emotions from love to contempt. "Here's my date. You're going to have to excuse us," she said with finality. She sat taller and smiled broadly at Nathan to convince Malcolm that this man was her Valentine, the new focus of her life.

Malcolm looked over his shoulder and up at Nathan, who studied him critically. He looked at Nathan as though he were trying to remember his face. But he clearly didn't associate him with the police officer who had ordered him away from Sabrina that night he tried to get her to listen to reason.

"How's it going, man?" Malcolm said in a cool tone to let Nathan knew he wasn't threatened by him. He extended his hand.

"Nathan, this is Malcolm. He was just leaving." Sabrina gave Malcolm a no-nonsense look.

Recognizing the man from their last encounter, Nathan didn't accept the man's offer of friendship. Instead, he slid his hand into his pocket and stared intently at the unwelcome intruder who had made Sabrina's lovely face pinch with tension.

Malcolm glowered at Nathan for his rejection. "Yeah, I was leaving. I only came to wish the lady a happy Valentine's Day." He took his time leaving the seat. "Have a good evening, 'Brina. I'm leaving town tomorrow morning, but you'll know where to reach me." He kissed her forehead, then sauntered across the room and back to the bar.

"I'm sorry about that," Sabrina said. She tried to ignore the tender feel of Malcolm's lips. She told herself it was all an act, a lie, only to get her back to support him financially again.

"No need to apologize. I could see that you didn't want to

be bothered. I guess he's having a hard time letting go."

The waitress finally appeared with their drinks.

Sabrina accepted her drink and took a few sips to rid her mouth of its dryness from her irritation. "I don't get it. I've made it clear to him that I'm through. Yet his ego won't allow him to accept this fact."

"I'm not trying to get into your business. But I have a feeling that in the past you've let him get by with a lot. Usually women will forgive a man anything as long as she doesn't know for sure he has been disrespectful to her."

"You're right, Nathan. I was one of those women who put up with half-truths and broken promises-all in the name of love. And then I had my work to occupy my mind. A lot of things I let go. I ignored the signals Malcolm was giving out because I have so much responsibility and stress, keeping up with my businesses. I trusted him. And he took advantage of me, knowing I didn't have time to keep tabs on him. But I'm all done with that, now that I know the kind of person and man he really is."

Nathan's eyes glinted with approval. He liked the idea of knowing that she was done with that creep. "Enough about him. We came to listen to the music and talk." He turned his attention toward the singer, who had begun another fabulous ballad.

Sabrina tried to concentrate on the woman, but when she looked over her shoulder, she saw Malcolm, sipping on his drink and giving her a longing glance. Sabrina moved her seat closer to Nathan. He smiled at her and draped his arm around her shoulder. Sabrina placed her hand on Nathan's knee and smiled at him the way she used to for Malcolm. She leaned close to Nathan and whispered how good the singer was and how glad she was that he had talked her into this wonderful evening out.

Nathan squeezed her shoulder; he looked as though she had said something much more meaningful than she had.

Sabrina stole a glance in Malcolm's direction, but he was nowhere to be seen. Her act had worked, she mused. She hoped her little performance had aggravated him and sent him away feeling hopeless and defeated as far as the two of them were concerned.

On the other hand, her flirtatious ways had gotten rid of one man, but encouraged another. Nathan took her hand in his warm one and intertwined his fingers with hers. He looked at her as though he was sure the evening had taken their friendship to another level.

It was Valentine's—a day for romance. Still feeling the sting of her broken relationship, Sabrina remained somewhat cynical. She wondered if love would always be an illusion for her.

But tonight, with her heart aching and her soul restless, she wished that romance could be a reality. She was a young woman with needs. And the men she'd known in her life had taught her that one didn't have to be in love to fulfill those needs. Looking into Nathan's smoldering eyes, she saw an invitation that her body was more than ready to accept.

Chapter Five

Sabrina had always known that she was somebody. She was independent financially, but like any healthy woman she wanted a man to care for her. She got lonely. Success wasn't something that she could cuddle up to when she ached for the strong arms of a man to make her feel alive, desired. For only one night, Sabrina wanted to be somebody's someone. And Nathan was the person she had chosen to fulfill her need.

Nathan had set off sparks in her with his quiet charm and that dazzling smile of his. On this Valentine's Day, she needed someone as sensitive and as kind as he to hold her and to kiss away all the loneliness that weighed like a burden in her heart. Being alone with Nathan, Sabrina experienced a cozy physical response that had lain dormant for months. She could also feel the negative effect that Malcolm had had on her at the club waning. She basked in the radiance of his wonderful smile and the serenely compelling look in his eyes.

When they arrived at Nathan's house, he showed her to his rec room. Though he would rather have taken her to his bedroom-his bed, he restrained his sexual anticipation. He didn't want to frighten her off and ruin a wonderful night that could wind up being the most memorable he had ever had in his life.

Nathan leaned close to Sabrina in his rec room while she attempted to play pool. He made an effort to teach her the techniques of shooting pool. His long, well-toned body fitted perfectly to Sabrina's shapely bent form. Brushing against her bottom, his manhood pulsated. Her sexy pose caused every nerve in his body to stand on end. His body hummed with lust.

He wanted to love every inch of her—love her all over. Her provocative posture was a passionate challenge. She glanced over her shoulder at him with a hint of a smile; her ebony eyes glimmering with mischief.

Nathan figured it would be best to ease into an intimate interlude with her. That way, she could feel as though she had control over the situation. He knew that she was threatened by situations where she didn't have the power.

After several failed attempts at hitting any of the billiard balls into the pockets, Sabrina admitted defeat. She placed her cue stick on the table. "That's it. I give up." She straightened and stretched, smiling. "This isn't the game for me."

Nathan couldn't take his eyes off her. He knew she wasn't aware of the captivating picture she made with that titillating smile of hers. His heart raced and his body ached with yearning. When she turned to face him, he eased up to her and fitted his arms around her waist, hoping she wouldn't flee from his touch. "You did fine for the first time. All you need is a few more lessons and you'll get the hang of it," he said softly as he gazed into her eyes.

"You mean there's hope for me?" A flash of humor crossed her face. She met the compelling look in his eyes and rested her hands on his chest. Her heart thumped with the desire that brewed in her veins. Hypnotized by his dreamy hazel eyes, she felt physical waves of wanting wash over her.

Nathan felt a ripple of mirth from her playful banter. He was thankful she hadn't shied away from him. He cupped her chin and placed a tender kiss upon her lips; it brought a sigh of surrender from her that pleased him.

The taste of his honey-like kiss shattered the stone around Sabrina's heart. Without any qualms, she looped her arms around his neck and parted her lips, inviting his eager tongue to caress hers.

Basking in the glory, the wonder of the moment, Nathan wanted to shout for joy. He was grateful that she was willing to let him do all the things he had dreamt of. Most astounding of all, she responded ardently. He ran his hands up and down her back, as though she were a fine-tuned instrument, a sleek saxophone with perfect pitch. As they grew more daring with their kisses and their touches, he loved the feel of her chest inhaling and exhaling against his torso.

Feeling the firm bulge of Nathan's arousal, Sabrina pressed her feminine mound upon it. The heat that settled there made her core wet with desire; her breath grew warm.

He showered kisses around her lips and along her jaw. He gripped her bottom and proceeded to sway back and forth against her until she moaned.

As she gave in to the overwhelming sensations of passion, her legs weakened. She gasped as she felt his hand slip beneath her skirt, caressing her thighs, her buttocks. Her arms moved from his neck to his broad shoulders so that she could layer his neck with feathery kisses. Eager for the taste of his lips, she planted her mouth over his sensuous lips. The strength of his arms encircling her turned her on. Lost in their deep kiss, she loosened his belt, unfastened his slacks and ripped down the zipper to free his proud manhood, which had taunted her, filled her with fiery curiosity. She reached for his engorged member and stroked it tenderly and ever so slowly.

She electrified him with her magnificent soft hands. Nathan's body grew rigid and his head fell back. He let out a groan; he teetered on his feet.

"Ah...Hmm...Sabrina. Please wait," he murmured and removed her hand. If he didn't, he feared he would embarrass himself by bursting in her hand. He pulled her into his arms and close to his chest again. She caressed his face and toyed with his earlobes, clouding his mind. "I want you. But are you sure this is what you want, too?" His voice was husky with lust. He palmed the side of her face and peered into her eyes, which were full of longing.

Sabrina removed one of his hands from her face and kissed the palm. "I want you, too. It would be a crime to leave and not finish what we've started, don't you think?" Staring at him, her ebony eyes glimmered with desire.

Mesmerized by the promise he saw revealed by her expression, he lifted her off the floor and hurried off to his bedroom.

Once he arrived and laid her out on the bed, he turned on the light. He wanted to see her face, her every action as she responded to the heated rapture of their intimacy. While he undid the delicate buttons on her silk blouse, he tickled her neck with tiny kisses. Pulling open her blouse, he placed his hand over one of her breasts and kneaded it. He placed a kiss where the globes rested together. He pressed his face between her naked breasts to savor their perfection; he flicked his tongue between her cleavage.

Sabrina shivered; she gripped his shoulders and whimpered with delight. Her center ached and grew swollen from the flames of passion that Nathan had stoked.

Lifting her skirt, Nathan tugged away her panties and tossed them onto the floor. He rested his hand on her stomach and eased his finger onto her feminine triangle. With one arm around her shoulder, he kissed and nibbled on her lips, while toying with the hair and the honey of her love essence. He ran his long fingers slowly up and down its sticky wetness until she felt a delightful glow that caused her breath to quicken. All the while he touched her, he was anxious to be inside her to enjoy the warmth of her there.

When Nathan abruptly rolled away from her, Sabrina felt vexed by the interruption in their love play. Yet she was pleased to see him hurriedly tearing away his clothes, and relieved to see him retrieve a condom from his nightstand drawer. He ripped away the foil and sheathed his erection.

Returning to bed, Nathan kissed her quivering stomach and dipped his tongue inside her navel. He dragged its tip around and in and out repeatedly.

Sabrina trembled and grew delirious with her exigent desire. The rasp of his tongue felt exquisite. She raised herself up to remove her blouse, which hung off her shoulders, while Nathan tugged her skirt over her hips. Once she was nude, he enfolded her in his arms and rolled her onto his chest. While they shared open-mouthed kisses, inhaling each other's hot breaths, he held her and dragged his warm hands up and down her curvy, fevered body. All the while, Sabrina was mindful of his shrouded, throbbing manhood between her thighs. Holding her tightly, Nathan maneuvered her onto her back and parted her legs. He pushed his firm, manly essence deep inside her.

At the thrill of their union, Sabrina exhaled with a loud moan. As he pumped leisurely and evenly inside her, she writhed against him. She gave in to the lush feelings that took her to a marvelous dimension. She yearned to hold on to the sweet sensations and the moments that were faultless. She couldn't remember when a man had made her feel more grateful to be feminine. Sabrina programmed Nathan's name in her heart with the excitement of his scattered kisses and ardent caresses. She was enraptured by all that he did and all that he was as a man.

As their journey of passion grew more intense, Nathan oohed and ahhed loudly. Sabrina's body jerked up and down with his lashing thrusts, which came harder and faster. Locking her arms around his waist, she rocked against him to quench her building need. Fire spread through her as he pounded his stomach against hers. Caught up in the throes of rapture, Sabrina trembled and felt as though she were blossoming. Feeling him erupt within her, she let out a lingering moan that revealed the complete satisfaction she had experienced.

"That was unbelievable," Nathan murmured against her face. He collapsed upon her, fondling her breasts. "And you looked utterly beautiful," he added in a breathless tone.

"I never imagined I'd end the day this way." She chuckled softly. Feeling as though she had been sedated, Sabrina caressed his arm and kissed the side of his face.

Nathan held her chin and kissed and licked her face, laughing low and sweetly. "This feels so right! I want this to be more than a one-night deal."

Sabrina touched his face, feeling full of wonder and joy. She relished the excitement that buzzed in her veins. The cozy warmth that she thought she'd never know again. "Is that what you really want?" She leaned toward him, resting her hand upon his chest.

"Oh yes! More than anything, my angel," he responded. He took her hand and kissed her fingertips.

She chuckled softly. "You're a thief. You've stolen your way into my heart. I'm not supposed to be ready for another relationship."

"Go with your heart." He placed his hand between her breasts where he could feel her heart beating. He removed his hand and kissed the place where he had felt delightful pounding.

Tears filled her eyes. He had convinced her. She encircled his neck to hold him.

Nathan slid his arm around her waist, tugged her back down beside him and cuddled her close to him. He nuzzled his face in her hair, then placed a kiss over an eyebrow. "You won't regret your decision."

Sabrina hugged Nathan. She caressed his torso; she relished the taut, smooth feel of his skin and the strength of his healthy body. "I should be getting home. But I'm not ready to leave."

He rubbed her ear with the back of his hand. "Stay. Tonight is special. It's our beginning. I want to wake up in the morning with you beside me, looking loved and happy." He traced her lips with the tip of his tongue, then pulled the folded comforter at the foot of the bed over their nude bodies. They snuggled together and fell asleep in each other's arms.

Nathan awakened alone in bed to the morning sun at the window. He had had an erotic dream of Sabrina, loving him. He was disappointed that she wasn't there at his side when he opened his eyes.

When he caught sight of her clothes draped on the chair across the room, he smiled in relief. It hadn't been a dream after all. The incredible, erotic evening had taken place.

He heard running water in the shower in the bathroom. A smile tilted the corners of his mouth and his passion rod grew rigid at the mere thought of Sabrina, standing nude and sudsy in the next room. He flung the covers off himself, bounded from the bed and hurried into the bathroom.

He stood in the doorway and listened to Sabrina, humming as though she were as happy as a lark on a spring day. He eased the shower door open; his eyes caressed the lushness of her body from head to toe. He wanted to be the soap that she glided over her delectable breasts and down her stomach and over her hips.

Turning to allow the water to rinse away the suds, Sabrina saw Nathan; her eyes revealed her pleasure at his appearance. "I didn't mean to wake you," she called above the spray of the water. She rinsed away the suds on her breasts and gave Nathan a teasing smile with a sparkle in her eyes.

His heart swelled with tenderness. Without saying a word, he stepped into the shower with her. He lifted her arms to fit over his shoulders and cornered her against the tiled wall as the warm water sprayed them. Holding on to her waist, he kissed her neck and ran his hands over her wet bottom, which bobbed delightfully with his touch.

Sabrina was thrilled by this escapade. Last night in his bedroom, she had been too enamored of his lovemaking to notice how well put together he was. Nathan's caramel body reminded her of the statue of Michelangelo's David. As far as she was concerned, Nathan had the same beauty and the same strong structure as the renowned piece of art. She welcomed his kisses, parting her lips and allowing his tongue to probe her mouth. Sucking on his tongue, she was ready for him again. She draped her arms around his neck and continued to kiss him while he unwrapped the condom he had palmed in his hand. When she saw the condom shrouding his engorged member, she allowed him to lift her legs around his waist. His maleness penetrated her with ease and invigorated her. She didn't mind the fact that her back rubbed uncomfortably against the tile or that her hair had gotten wet. All her discomforts were forgotten. Her only concerns were Nathan's luscious thrusts, and the way she felt and the satisfaction on his face. As their exhilaration mounted to a full, body-shuddering climax, their moans and groans grew louder and echoed off the walls. At the end of the interlude, Nathan lifted her legs from around his waist and set her feet carefully on the shower floor. He retrieved the soap and proceeded to slowly suds her all over.

Giggling with pleasure from the glow and the warmth of the new feelings that had evolved between them, Sabrina confiscated the soap from him and lathered him, too. They stood beneath the shower, hugging and kissing until all the suds had been rinsed off.

"I can't wait for the next holiday," Nathan said, tossing aside the large towel he had used to dry off Sabrina and himself. He sat on the bed and watched Sabrina as she used his blow dryer to put the finishing touches on styling her hair.

"And to think it all started on New Year's She smiled in the mirror at Nathan, who watched her every move as though she was a marvel. "I don't remember much from that night...other than that I was an emotional wreck." Her voice wavered. She turned toward him but was unable to look him in the eyes. "Every time I think of that night and how irresponsibly I acted...well, I feel embarrassed."

Nathan came to her, held her by the shoulders and gazed into her liquid ebony eyes. The look of shame he saw there made him guilty for the hoax he had pulled on her. "You have nothing to be embarrassed over, Sabrina. Nothing happened that night, other than me just sleeping in the same bed with you. I mean, I stayed the night in your bed, but I did nothing more than sleep."

She felt stunned and furious; her warm expression grew distorted. "What are you saying, Nathan?" She stepped back from him.

"Before you attack me, hear me out," he implored. Never

in his whole life had he been so humbled by anything he had done. "You were awful to me that night at the party. You humiliated me. You were obnoxious. I had been able to live with the way you'd belittle me at the Center during staff meetings, concerning the activities I'd recommend for the kids. I pretended not to care about the cold shoulder you'd been giving me from day one, since I was introduced to you. So what if you turned up your cute nose at me like I wasn't good enough for you to share a casual conversation with, I used to tell myself. There were plenty of other women who found me charming. I didn't need you. But you had to go shoot your mouth off at the party as if I was to blame for whatever it was that made you drunk. And I'd had enough. I'd had my share of drinks like you, and my judgment became clouded. I'm ashamed of what I did. I've never done anything like it before. I played a very bad joke on you. And I'm sorry."

She gave him a hostile glare. "Tell me, what in the world did I say to make you humiliate me like you did?" She threw the words at him like stones. Rancor sharpened her voice.

"Crossover Brother. You attacked me and embarrassed me. You accused me of not liking or respecting black women. I love black women. Just because you'd seen me out with women of another race doesn't mean I don't have any respect or don't like sisters." He searched her face for signs of penitence. Her depressed mood had brought out the insensitivity and irrational behavior. "I know I went too far, but I couldn't resist it. That night, all I wanted to do was to knock you off that high cloud you always appear to be floating on."

Should she let yesterday's cloud smother the sunshine that lay before her with this man? she wondered, feeling full of remorse. She didn't like what he had told her she had said. The slur had been uncalled for. It was something that a person who had no class would do. And she certainly considered herself a woman with more sensibility and morals than to hurt anyone intentionally. Too much champagne, too much pain had been the cause of her spewing the slurs to Nathan. Black men who favored white women were a topic that she and other black women spoke about in private, but didn't dare to verbalize openly. Most bore their frustration in silence. Like her black girlfriends, Sabrina loved and admired black men. And it always hurt to see them enchanted with "other" women. There were too few good black men for single black women, and the idea of white women making the odds worse for black women to find "Mr. Right" was a sore point. Whenever a black woman saw a black man out with a white woman, it was a source of pain and envy. They didn't have to know the particular black man personally to feel the slight. And Sabrina, like most black women, wondered why it was that brothers couldn't find a pearl within their race instead of crossing over. It told the women that they weren't bright enough, beautiful enough or classy enough to measure up to white women, Sabrina knew. Black men who chose to date white women didn't understand the resentment or the pain of black women and probably never would, Sabrina thought. They wrote off the reaction to interracial dating as just the bad attitude of the sister. Even more reason to cross over.

But none of this could excuse her rudeness to Nathan that night. "I apologize for my awful slur. I had more to drink than I could handle. Your personal life and your preferences are no business of mine. But you did go too far with your prank. Nathan, you undressed me and climbed into my bed, and even spent the night with me." Her face crinkled with renewed anger. "I could ruin you. You're aware of that?"

"Yes, I know." His eyes harbored his regret and shame.

"You took advantage of me," she said. Her voice carried an edge of indignation. "You're an officer of the law and..."

"Hold on. Hear me out. I was wrong and I regretted it once I saw how upset you were that morning. But I had too much pride to let you know I'd done such a thing. And uh...I sort of liked the power the situation gave me." He appeared smug. "Big, bad Sabrina Lewis was all shook up because she thought I'd broken down her perfect facade." His composure gave way to an imploring half-smile. "It was adolescent and I hope you can forgive me."

Sabrina tried to hide her melting reaction to that gentle, affectionate look she saw in his eyes. He didn't deserve to be let off the hook just yet. "You're awful, Nathan. I shouldn't have a thing to do with you!"

Seeing her reaction, Nathan was mortified. But he was glad that he had finally told her the truth. He felt as though a weight had been lifted off him. "I deserve a punishment, but I hope you won't be too dastardly. I was a desperate man using desperate means to get close to a woman I've wanted to get to know for quite some time," he said in a soft, apologetic tone. "I never touched you. I was tempted, but I'm not that much of a creep. You see, I wanted yo u to want me like you did last night. It was certainly more meaningful." He lavished her with a divine smile.

Pensively, Sabrina ran her hand through her freshly dried hair. She thought of the sweet love Nathan had given her. She had felt beautiful, desirable in his arms. Her intimate interlude couldn't have been more perfect. The simple touch of his hand had made her feel enchanted.

Nathan regarded her with open fondness. He brushed his fingertip down the middle of her nose and smiled. "Sabrina, that night is gone. Like I said, I'll never do anything like that again. I promise. I like to think I've earned your trust and affection."

Sabrina stared at him intently. "You're forgiven this time. Only because you have earned my affection—even my respect. I'm glad you told me what really happened. It's a relief to know that I'm not such a hussy after all." She chuckled.

"Now that that is cleared up, come here, woman. Let me hold you." He swooped her into his embrace and kissed her. "The games are over. You can count on me being straightfor-ward and honest." He kissed her again.

She accepted his kisses and smiled at him. She was ready to move past this incident on to building a strong relationship based on honesty, respect and mutual affection.

Hugging Sabrina, Nathan felt a sense of relief and pleasure. Nothing meant more to him than her forgiveness. He wanted to live his life making her smile, making her laugh, and making her want him more with each passing day.

"Nathan, playtime is over." She laughed softly. "You must take me home. I have to change clothes. I have some things I need to attend to at home."

"Sure thing, lady. But you have to promise to have dinner with me this evening. I'll do all the cooking. All I require is your company."

"Hmm...that sounds fabulous. I can't resist that." She winked at him and took him by the hand to leave the paradise they had created in his bedroom.

Nathan whistled while he prepared dinner for himself and Sabrina. His simple menu consisted of baked potatoes, salad, and a steak he would cook to her liking. He had gone to the gourmet bakery and bought cheesecake for dessert. Sabrina had mentioned that was a favorite of hers. Taking the cake out of the cardboard box and placing it in the fridge, he hoped that Sabrina would be in a romantic mood and decide that he would be her dessert. The cheesecake would be even more delicious shared in bed after they had made love. As he checked the kitchen table he had set, the doorbell chimed. He rushed to the door to greet the delightful object of his affection. Sabrina.

"Daddy!"

Nathan's mouth fell open when he saw his darling daughter, Amber. He dropped to his knees to hug and kiss her. His heart felt as though it would burst with the love he felt for the eight-year-old he hadn't seen in nearly two years because of her mother's selfishness and callousness. He held Amber at arm's length and studied her adorable, light-complexioned face and her hazel eyes, which matched his. He touched her curly light brown hair as if he couldn't believe she was actually there with him. The child looked more as though she was of Italian or Jewish background than the offspring of a Southern Caucasian woman and an African-American male.

"Hello, Nathan," said a woman standing behind Amber, in a cool tone. "You're certainly looking good as ever."

He had been so enthralled by his daughter that he hadn't noticed when his wife appeared.

Nathan glared up into the face of his ex-wife, Caroline. He gathered Amber in his arms and stood up. "Hello, Caroline. I'm glad you finally came to your senses," he said icily. "It's so good to see my baby-at last." He beamed at Amber, whose arm was affectionately draped around his neck.

The blonde woman with the cool blue eyes studied Nathan with a hint of a smile. "She's been asking about you. She's been driving me crazy to see you. I thought it was time to set aside our differences for her." Caroline reached out, stroked Amber's hair and smiled at her.

"I'm glad you decided to do the right thing." Nathan kissed his daughter on the cheek. When he saw the taxi driver bringing two large suitcases toward his place, he looked to Caroline for an explanation.

"I thought Amber and I could stay for a while. There's so much that you and I need to talk about, work through. Of course, it's for Amber's best interest. She's at the age where she needs to know her father."

"You want me to leave these out here, ma'am?" said the hefty taxi driver impatiently.

"No, you can bring them in, please," Caroline said, sauntering past Nathan and Amber as if she had been invited and had come home from a long, tiring trip.

Though Nathan remained affable to Caroline for his daughter's sake, he had to bridle the anger that consumed his being. He cursed silently. The moment Sabrina assessed this unexpected situation, he knew that the small, cozy bond that they had just formed would certainly be broken. He decided to call Sabrina and cancel their evening. He wanted to talk to her and explain everything without thrusting it upon her. He had nearly closed the door, when he caught a glimpse of Sabrina pulling her car up in front of his house. His heart sank with despair.

Chapter Six

Easing her car in front of Nathan's place after a long day of handling her businesses, Sabrina felt like a teenager meeting her date for the high school prom. All through the day, erotic images of Nathan had played in her mind. She had grown warm and tingly, thinking of the way he had caressed her and made her body hum with pleasure.

Sabrina caught a glimpse of Nathan in his doorway and her soul radiated with an excitement she had never experienced before. Exiting her parked car and walking toward him in the dusk of the February day, Sabrina felt as if she walked on winged feet. Was she over-reacting to this man too soon to fill the void left in her life by ended romance? The closer she got to Nathan in his doorway, the more she noticed how affected his smile was and how weary his eyes were.

Opening his door wide, Nathan greeted her with a brief kiss while his arms encircled her, one hand on the small of her back.

Feeling his lips on hers stirred a sweet, cozy feeling within Sabrina. She returned his embrace and savored the feel of his body close to hers. She was all set to draw the kiss out until she spotted a little white girl in the hallway, sizing them up.

"You have company, I see," Sabrina said. The girl with the wavy hair piqued Sabrina's interest. Perhaps Nathan's partner and his family were waiting. She knew the two officers were close.

"Yeah, sort of. Come here, sweetheart," Nathan called to the little girl.

The child, who seemed to be about eight, eyed Sabrina suspiciously and didn't respond to Nathan's request.

"Amber. Please come and meet my friend," he said in a soothing tone. "She's a nice lady."

Amber twisted her mouth in that way children do when they don't want to do something, than ambled toward Nathan.

"Sabrina, this is my daughter, Amber. Amber, this is Miss Lewis."

Sabrina stood there blank and amazed by what he had just disclosed to her. "Hello," Sabrina said faintly. It was all she could manage. She chided herself for not taking the time to learn any personal details of Nathan's life. She had been so swept away by their passion and the romance that her reasoning had been clouded. Studying the gorgeous child, Sabrina could see that she was obviously biracial. The mother no doubt was white. The undeniable fact raised that issue of the black male, white woman conflict to her mind. Sabrina didn't want to feel resentment of the stunning news about Nathan that had just been presented to her. But she did. It was one thing to accept the fact that he had dated white women, but to know that he had the lifetime bond of a child with a white woman presented a whole new set of problems for Sabrina. If she chose to continue her relationship with Nathan, could she be open-minded enough to accept his biracial daughter and the relationship that he would probably have to maintain with his daughter's mother?

Nathan watched Sabrina watching his Amber. Her face gave no clue to what she was thinking. Surely she wouldn't dare shun his affection or his attention because he had a biracial child. Hopefully, he wouldn't be pushed to make a choice. He didn't want to lose Sabrina, but if she couldn't accept his daughter, she wasn't the kind of woman he needed.

Sabrina tried to minimize Amber's ethnicity. She wanted to be fair and reasonable in this situation. After all, Nathan was no ordinary man. The thing of it was that she hadn't dated men with kids. Kids created too many complications in a relationship. And, to her, men with children—especially those

who had never married—were a turn-off. She had no respect
for men who bred children and didn't hang around to be a
proper father. She'd grown up without knowing her own
father. But the pride on Nathan's face showed her that he was
a good father and not one of those walk-away kind like her
own had been.

"This is my little princess," Nathan said, patting his daughter's hair. "She's here to spend a few days."

"How nice," Sabrina said. She gave him an insipid smile.

Sabrina thought how she had rushed through her busy day,
hoping to have an intimate evening of conversation and
romance and passion. She certainly hadn't expected to be hit
over the head with an introduction of a child—his child. She
was irritated and miserable by the turn of events.

Amber wedged her body between Sabrina and Nathan, who
stood close together. She hadn't bothered to say hello to
Sabrina. "Is she going to stay for dinner, too?" Amber gave
her father a hostile look.

Nathan gazed at Sabrina, then he regarded his daughter.
"Will you excuse us, dear? You can go on and get started with
your meal before it gets cold. Uh...we'll be in a minute."

He whirled his insolent daughter away from him and
coaxed her in the direction of the kitchen. Then he turned to
Sabrina. "Let's not stand here. Come into the living room.
I'm sure you have plenty of questions. And there are some
things I have to share with you. Things you should know," he
said, taking Sabrina's hand and leading her into the living
room.

A flicker of apprehension coursed through her. As far as
she was concerned, the evening was ruined and couldn't be
salvaged with anything he could say at this point.

"I had a great evening in mind for us," Nathan said ruefully. "As you can see, our plans are going to be altered with the
presence of my daughter. I had no idea she was coming..."

"Nathan! Amber told me we had company." A blonde
woman breezed into the room as if Nathan's place was her
home as well. She narrowed her blue eyes at the two who

Nathan blinked excessively at the blonde's sudden appearance. "Sabrina, this is...Caroline."

"Hi, I'm Amber's mom and Nathan's ex-wife," Caroline volunteered with a false tone of pleasure. She used her hand to flick her long hair over her shoulder. She smiled smugly. She seemed proud to be able to reveal this information to Sabrina

Nathan's white woman, Sabrina thought. Once again that ugly feeling of envy coursed through her. He had married and shared a child with this woman who was sizing her up. Was a relationship with him worth dealing with this kind of baggage of his? She felt a twinge of betrayal. She had given this man a precious part of herself only to find that she had complicated her life even more than it had been with Malcolm. She really didn't want to be caught up in this drama. But she had laid her emotions on the line with Nathan when she had slept with him.

Sabrina noticed the defiant look Caroline gave her. She returned the look. She wasn't about to let this woman intimidate her. She was just as good or better than Caroline was. Blue eyes and blonde hair didn't make her superior to her. Caroline was pleasant to look at, even though she appeared to be twenty or thirty pounds overweight. She reminded Sabrina of those aristocratic women she'd seen in magazines. Sabrina recognized Amber's features on this woman. Amber was a slightly tanned version of her mother.

Caroline gave Sabrina a superior smirk. "Are you staying for dinner, Sabrina? You're quite welcome. As usual, Nathan has prepared a delicious meal. And plenty of it. His cooking is one of many things I've missed, being away from him," she said. She gave Nathan a fond look.

Caroline took a seat on the arm of the sofa near Sabrina and Nathan in the living room. She crossed her legs as though she had been invited to share this moment, this conversation.

Sabrina was disturbed and disquieted by the woman's intrusion. "No, thank you. I just remembered I have some things that require my attention," Sabrina lied. "Since you've just dropped into town, I certainly wouldn't want to interfere.

Enjoy your evening." She gave the woman a cool smile. "Nice meeting you," Sabrina added curtly and sauntered to the front door.

What a fool she'd been, Sabrina thought, making her way to the door. Nathan was no different than any other man who had come into her life only to disappoint her. He had pulled that awful hoax on her and charmed her into forgiving him. He had tricked her into thinking they had slept together to get her attention because he cared for her. Her blood sizzled with anger. But now she was convinced that the deal with him had been that he only wanted to seduce her to remind himself of what it was like to be with a sister. She felt used and she didn't like the feeling—not one bit. Hadn't she vowed only a few months ago not to be taken advantage of again by any member of the male species? Her loathing for Nathan welled like bile in her stomach.

"Sabrina, I'm sorry. I can't blame you for leaving," he said. His voice was strained. "Caroline and Amber were the last people I expected to show up today." He caught hold of Sabrina's hand, but she snatched it away. His eyes took on a haunted, anxious look at her response to his touch. "Oh Sabrina, this visit is about my daughter, Amber. Nothing more," he assured her, searching her eyes for empathy. "I'll call you later when I can talk. And don't jump to any conclusions about slowing down our thing." He cupped her chin and lunged forward to kiss her.

Sabrina slapped away his hand and glared at him. She whirled away from Nathan and stalked out of his house. It was over! It had to be, she reasoned, feeling her face growing hot with anger.

It was nearly closing time at Romantic Poses. Sabrina stared out the window at the cold, dreary day. She watched as the people on the street hustled in and out of the businesses near her with their shoulders hunched against the cold, blowing clouds of frigid air while they talked with each other.

Though it was blustery, Sabrina thought what a wonderful night it could have been if Nathan were free. They could have spent the evening snuggled together in front of a cozy fire at her house, talking and making sweet, tender love. Sabrina shivered at the thought of lovemaking with Nathan. She blinked several times to wipe away the images that would never be. It had been days since she had seen Nathan. It suited her just fine with the company he had, she thought defiantly and swallowed her regret.

"These are great!" exclaimed Kathy Mason. She studied the proofs of her mother's, Phyllis Graham's pictures. "She looks like a totally different woman. Oh Sabrina, everyone will be tickled with joy when they see how gorgeous Mama looks."

"Camille is a genius. I was fortunate to nab her. And to think the sister couldn't find a job with her credentials from college in photo-journalism. She is gifted in giving women that soft yet dignified, beautiful image. Her pictures never come out with that harsh, drab look I've seen at other places. I'm going to try to keep her as long as I can. Hopefully, the salary I plan to increase will keep her dedicated to Romantic Poses. I intend to open another place like this one in a few years. I'd like for her to train the other photographers as well."

"I know which of these poses I like. But it's up to Mama to make the final selection," Kathy said as she shuffled through the proofs for the third time. "How are things between you and Nathan? Is it getting any hotter?" Interest and amusement flickered in her eyes.

"There's nothing to tell. I decided to leave Nathan Atkins alone," she informed her friend. Sabrina left the window and sorted a stack of photo envelopes, checking out proofs that had been taken during the week.

Kathy gave her friend a questioning look. "Say what?"

"It no big deal. He's just another man. I should have had my head examined for getting caught up in a 'thing' with Nathan in the first place. I wish I had taken time to talk with him about his personal life. But that overwhelming physical chemistry between us left no time for reasoning, thinking."

Kathy frowned at her and her puzzling comment. "What are you talking about? You've been the kind of woman who has always been too serious, too up-tight. It was good to see you throw caution to the wind and just let down your inhibitions, and go for it with someone as sweet as Nathan."

"Yeah, it was nice," she said wistfully. Then she cleared her throat. "But I've paid a price for throwing caution to the wind. Just as I was all set to move whatever we had going to another level, he surprise me with an eight-year-old daughter and an ex-wife who happens to be blonde with blue eyes."

"No lie! I had no idea Nathan had been married. I only met him through my husband when Nathan came here a few years ago." Kathy's eyes danced with the juicy revelation. "I knew he dated white women and all, but I had no idea he had married one. What a downer." She gave her friend an understanding look. "I would have reacted like you did, learning something like that out of the blue."

"I met his ex-wife and his daughter a week ago. They've come to Hunter's Creek for a visit. I don't know what the deal is with that. I didn't bother to ask. Learning he even had a daughter and had been married dampened things for me." Sabrina shrugged. She fingered her gold necklace pensively and tried to minimize the disappointment she felt.

Kathy shook her head in dismay. "I'm sorry, girl. I thought sure Nathan would help you regain your faith in men and romance."

She let out a choked, desperate laugh. "Well, he didn't. He and I were getting along well until I learned of his past. His ex-wife acts like most white women with brothers. You know that touch of arrogance they give off to try to make you feel less than they are." Sabrina remembered the look Caroline had given her. It was a victorious look that said: it's over now that I'm back and in control.

"Don't you want to see him? Speak to him?" Kathy leaned on the counter and eyed Sabrina.

Sabrina wouldn't hold her friend's gaze. "Nope. It's better this way."

Kathy frowned and let out a sigh. "Here we go again," she said, clearly thinking of the incident with Malcolm. "Every time something unpleasant happens in your personal life you shut it out and refuse to discuss it. That's no way of dealing with your problems."

"I handle things the best way I can, okay?" Sabrina snapped. "I have my businesses to run. They're the only things that I can count on for security. I can't lose my focus on them because of the foolishness of a man."

"But the older you get, the more problems like these are bound to arise. The men you'll come in contact with will either have kids or be divorced. You're going to have to learn to compromise and be part of the real world if you don't want to end up lonely. Face it, Sabrina," she chided. "Good men can make just as many bad choices and mistakes as women can. What matters is the way they face their problems and take responsibility for their actions."

"I don't have any more patience with Nathan than I did with Malcolm." She spoke with grave deliberation.

"Oh, Malcolm's stuff is not to be excused." Kathy pursed her lips as though she tasted something bitter. "He was a creep! I told you I suspected he was nothing but a user, but you wouldn't listen. You were mesmerized by his ability to make you laugh. He charmed you enough to get you to go to the bank. I don't know how he did it, but he did. And you went grinning all the way with him."

Sabrina's body stiffened with indignation. "I believe Malcolm really cared for me before he went to live in New York," she said defensively. She straightened the magazines in the waiting area as though she wished Kathy and her prying would go away. "Both of us knew what it's like not to have anything. We're survivors. We refuse to give in to the odds against us."

"Making money was about the only thing you two really had in common," Kathy said with a sarcastic laugh.

Sabrina shook her head in annoyance. "It wasn't just the

money. He had a dream of being a successful entertainer. And I always wanted to be more than what I came from. My goodness! What's wrong with that?"

Kathy licked her lips as though their disagreement had made her thirsty. She went to the coffeemaker for a cup of coffee. "Nothing is wrong with that. But since you started your career, you've been obsessed with these businesses. You've forgotten how to enjoy life and how to socialize. You're certainly not the same person I've known since we were teens. You're becoming hard and cold and I don't want to see that happening to you."

Sabrina wanted understanding from her friend and not the tongue lashing she was receiving. "I...I have had no one to depend on but myself. You know that. I refuse to live the way my mother did. She was content being a waitress and making her way with the help of the men who have been in and out of her life through the years. I've seen the way men have used my mother, trifled with her emotions, treated her like she was nothing. I was the one who had to suffer for her lack of attention, her depression when a 'romance' fell apart. I was the one who had to suffer the gossip over her loose ways. I was the one guys thought would be a clone of Grace. I had to show people in this town that I was more. Ever since the day I graduated from vocational school in cosmetology, I was determined that I was going to use that skill to turn my life around three-hundred-sixty degrees." Sabrina plopped down on the sofa with a loud thud and a look of exasperation.

"Okay. I know this. And you've worked hard and you're to be commended for all that you have done for someone your age. But Sabrina, it's time to pull back some. You should find someone you can trust to share what you have, or else everything you've gained is meaningless."

"So what you're saying is that I'm supposed to overlook the fact that Nathan is divorced from a white woman and has a biracial daughter who is living at his house?" Sabrina's eyes were stony with anger.

"You need to talk to the man. You need to listen to what he

has to say," Kathy said with concern. "So what if he was married to a white woman? She is his ex now and he has shown sincere interest in you." She sighed with frustration. "You're supposed to be this savvy businesswoman, but when it comes to life, you're clueless." Kathy returned to the counter. "I want to get another look at Mama's pictures. I just know she isn't going to pick the one I like best. I'm going to place an order for some of my own."

Sabrina didn't like Kathy's criticism. She thought of the messages that Nathan had left on her machine in the last couple of days, which she had ignored. He had told her he had to work and that he was busy because of his houseguests. However, he wanted her to call him, so they could get together and have a long talk about everything. Sabrina had erased the messages and had attempted to wipe him from her memory as well. It was useless to talk, she figured. All she had left were memories of the hot, steamy night of passion they'd shared. And those memories seemed to have an enduring life no matter what she did to smother them.

Sabrina's reverie was broken by the sound of the door of Romantic Poses opening. She bounded from her seat to greet her customer. She was surprised to see a somber-looking Nathan Atkins.

"Ladies," Nathan said, removing his gloves. He smiled cursorily.

Sabrina was smitten by his good looks. But the reasons why she had chosen not to be bothered with him came to mind. She regarded him with a lofty expression and didn't speak.

"Hey, Nathan. It's good to see you," Kathy said in a cheery tone. "I haven't seen you since my party." She swung her gaze to Sabrina to check out her attitude now that Nathan had shown up.

"I've been working and busy," he explained. "How's that husband of yours?" He stole a glance at Sabrina, who busied herself behind the counter.

"He's kicking. The high school basketball team consumes his time. You know how snarly he can get during the season."

Kathy chuckled.

Though he chatted with Kathy, Nathan surreptitiously eyed Sabrina with interest as she proceeded to fan through her appointment book. It bothered him that she was nonchalant to his presence. When she sashayed from behind the counter to put out her new brochures and then walked back past him, he took in her appearance. Her skirt was short and showed off her magnificent legs. Just for a moment, flashes of what those legs had felt like, intertwined with his during lovemaking, stirred him with desire.

"Miss Lewis, how are you today?" he asked stiffly, walking toward her. He couldn't stand her ignoring him any longer. She had had a week to think over the personal details in his life; he had come to set things right or to see where he stood with her. He tried not to think that what they had begun would be ended so soon. But if she chose to be that small-minded, he would have to learn to live with it and move on with his life. Deep in his heart he hoped that Sabrina would open her mind and accept the things she knew about him.

Sabrina turned a cold eye on him. "I'm fine. Just fine," she answered icily. "What can I do for you?" she asked in her businesslike voice.

"I came to talk. You and I must talk." He stared at her intently.

Kathy gave Sabrina a warning look. "Hey, I'd love to stay and chat with you guys. But I have a couple of errands to run before rushing home to prepare dinner for my sweetie." She returned the proofs of her mother to their envelop, set them aside and slipped into her coat. She went to Sabrina and pulled her aside, giving Nathan a smile. "Excuse us." She held on to Sabrina's arm. "Listen to the man. He cares about you. I can see his interest for you written all over his face. Be nice," she said in a warning whisper before releasing her friend.

"Bye, Nathan. Take care," Kathy called in a cheery voice, breezing out the door and into the chill of the evening.

Sabrina and Nathan stood staring at each other. The tension between them could have been cut with a knife.

"As lovely as you are, I didn't come here to stare at you," Nathan said. "I want to know why you have shut me out, Sabrina."

"I can't compete with your family. I thought it was best for me to let you handle your responsibilities without any distractions." She gave a wary shrug and attempted to maintain a pose of total unconcern.

"There's no competition," Nathan said. "I have a daughter. I love her and intend to give her the attention and whatever else she needs. My ex-wife is just that—ex. She is due my respect for my daughter's sake even though I don't have feelings for her. So I can't understand why you appear to be so threatened by something that I have to be accountable for." He gave her a challenging look.

"I've been through the emotional grinder once. I don't have the strength to be disappointed, or toyed with again." Her voice wavered.

"Sabrina, sweetheart, I wouldn't dare ask anything of you that you aren't ready to give. I care about you. I had plans to show you how much until destiny brought Amber back into my life. The timing is wrong, but I can deal with her and you. All I'm asking is that you give me a chance. It's a shame to discover how right we are and then just let such precious emotions wither." His voice was soft, seductive.

All of her loneliness and confusion welded together in one upsurge of devouring yearning for him. The man she had become fond of. She leaned on the counter to still her heart, which had begun to race. She wanted him. Yes, she did. But she just couldn't let go of her pride to admit it.

Nathan approached her reluctantly. His brow furrowed at her silence. "I came here today to remind you of that museum field trip you arranged for that exhibit commemorating Black History month. The director called to confirm our request for the group."

Sabrina grew flustered at the mention of the kids and the Center. The last thing she wanted was to renege on her responsibility as a mentor. "Don't worry. I will be there for the trip," she assured him. "I'd never let them down." She raised her chin and assumed all the dignity she could muster.

He inclined his head in a gesture of entreaty. "But what about me? Where do you and I go from this point, Sabrina?"

Sabrina shrugged to hide her confusion and wondered if she could rid herself of the unreasonable resentment she had for Caroline. And was she woman enough to share Nathan with the demanding attention of his young daughter? "Wouldn't it be much easier for us to go our separate ways and just remain friends?" She managed a tremulous smile.

"It's not that easy any more for me, Sabrina," he said. Desire glowed in his eyes. "You're emblazoned in my heart and my mind."

With a deliberate, casual movement, she allowed her eyes to meet his warm gaze. The stone center of her heart cracked and the delicate flower of her affection for him blossomed. A tender smile broke through her mask of uncertainty.

That simple yet endearing action was all Nathan needed. A grin overtook his features. He breathed a sigh of relief. He had been reprieved.

Chapter Seven

The morning of the Center trip to the museum, Nathan called Sabrina and asked her to stop at his house before she went to the center. She tried to get out of the chore, but since the visit involved paperwork for the outing, Sabrina agreed. He had the list with the names of the kids who were allowed to go on the Museum trip.

When Sabrina arrived at Nathan's house and rang the doorbell, she prayed that he would answer the door. She didn't want to deal with Caroline's snootiness. Her prayer wasn't fulfilled. Caroline came to the door, her blonde hair wet; she was wrapped in one of Nathan's robes. Her complexion was pink as if she had come out of the shower. Caroline gave Sabrina a forced smile. She eyed her as though she were a pesky door-to-door solicitor.

"Nathan asked me to come by for the trip list," Sabrina said. She smiled smoothly, betraying none of the annoyance that Caroline's take-over presence at Nathan's house aroused in her. She hated having to explain herself to this woman to whom she owed no explanations.

"Nathan told me to listen out for you. He's in the shower. Come in and I'll get him. We overslept this morning." Caroline flashed her a superior grin. She held the door open to allow Sabrina's entrance. Then she turned away and headed for Nathan's bedroom. She entered without knocking, Sabrina noticed. Sabrina was left standing alone in the foyer, feeling awkward and wishing she was somewhere else. From where she stood, she glimpsed Caroline leaving Nathan's room with

94

a smile.

"He'll be right with you," Caroline said, disappearing into the kitchen.

Nathan appeared dressed in a robe as well. A towel was draped around his neck and his hair still glistened with water.

The sight of his attire reminded Sabrina of their own sexy, passionate shower interlude. Had he and Caroline been up to the same thing? Had Caroline burst into the bathroom to catch a glimpse of him naked? she wondered, not forgetting how casually the woman had entered his bedroom.

Recognizing the pinched look on Sabrina's face, Nathan figured that she had grown suspicious at seeing the two of them still in their robes. "Caroline and Amber share a bedroom and a bathroom. I have a bedroom and a bathroom to myself," he said quickly to appease her.

"You don't owe me any explanations. What goes on in your house is your business," she said in a tone of indifference.

"There's nothing going on," he said in exasperation. "I thought sure I had gained your trust. I thought you and I had gotten past this issue." He searched her face for the signs of faith he needed from her.

The look in Sabrina's eye was cold and hard. "The list, Nathan," she demanded, easing her mouth into a skeptical smile. It was too early to deal with her annoyance at how comfortable he and Caroline were under the same roof. She supposed that once one had been married, it was easy as pie to fall back into the intimate familiarity that they had once shared in marriage.

He reached into the pocket of his robe, pulled out a white envelope and handed it to her. "Thanks for coming by for this," Nathan said. He smiled at her, disregarding her somber expression. "The required list is in there. I'm going to have to run by police headquarters and check in with the sarge before coming to the Center. I thought we could save time if you had the list to check off the names of the kids who have parental permission. I should get to the Center right before the bus is supposed to pull out." He kept watching her and smiling. But his attempt to get a warm look from Sabrina was futile.

"Well, I'm off. You should be getting dressed to get started for your day," she said sarcastically. She tucked the envelope with the list into her coat pocket. She wasted no further time in conversation; she turned quickly and was out the door before he could say any more.

When she returned to her car, she noticed that Nathan still watched her from the door. She didn't bother to look directly his way. She didn't want him to see how jealous she really was that he and his ex were running around each other half-dressed as though they were still married.

"I want this fooling around to stop! I want every behind in a seat. I want you to close your mouths!" Sabrina stood in the aisle of the field-trip bus. Her hazel complexion was tinged red from her frustration amidst the chaos on the bus.

The kids from the Hubbard Community Center didn't respond right away. This aggravated Sabrina even more. She wished that Nathan was here. He would have been able to quiet them just by his appearance and that no-nonsense look in his eyes.

Sabrina looked for assistance to the bus driver, Mr. Young, but he showed no interest in her problem. He shook his head at the kids' rowdy behavior and continued to study the sports page of the newspaper.

"Pizza! We'll go by the Pizza Hut after the museum. All you can eat," she promised. "That is, if you settle down and behave," she shouted above the hubbub.

Everyone froze in their various antics of misbehavior. Quiet order fell over the bus.

"That's better," she said, feeling relieved that her bargain had worked. "We'll be on our way as soon as Mr. Nate gets here."

Sabrina wished she hadn't decided to get the kids into the bus before Nathan arrived. But being the organized person that she was, she thought that it would save time to be all set and ready to leave.

It was a cold, blustery February day; Sabrina glanced at her watch, then toyed with the collar on her thick, woolen coat. She considered telling the bus driver to leave. She tried to be patient, knowing that Nathan was tardy because of official business with his job. And the thought of dealing with thirty kids all alone at their destination further convinced her to wait a little longer. She wasn't a superwoman. There was no way she could deal with all these kids alone. She was relieved when she finally saw Nathan's black Maxima zooming onto the Hubbard Center parking lot and easing into a vacant spot.

"Hey Miss Lewis, who is that little white girl with Mr. Nate?" fifteen-year-old Charmaine, a member of Sabrina's teen group at the Center, asked. She sat behind Sabrina. Charmaine and the other teen girls peered out their windows with interest.

Nathan rushed toward the bus with Amber in tow. The sight irked Sabrina. Had a last minute decision to bring his daughter been an added cause for his delay and their tardiness for their destination? she fumed. And her with a busload of restless teens waiting. She had accepted his work excuse. But she imagined him wasting precious time persuading a stubborn Amber to come with them. She was full of dread, knowing that the trip was going to be even more challenging with his bothersome child along. It was bad enough to be responsible for the teens, whom she had prepped with a lecture on the proper behavior expected of them on this public outing. But to have spoiled Amber along presented even more problems. The girl was so much younger than the other kids. There was no way that Nathan could chaperone properly with his young daughter along; she would require his full attention. Amber would be nothing but trouble, fumed Sabrina.

"Sorry I'm so late," Nathan said, lifting Amber to the top step of the bus. She was bundled in a pink coat and a matching knit hat. Nathan helped his daughter onto a seat behind the bus driver. Standing in the aisle, he greeted and counted the kids who had come. "Great. No one backed out."

"Who is that little girl?" Charmaine asked Nathan, studying the child who watched her father's every move.

Smiling at Amber, Nathan went to stand beside her. "Ladies and gentlemen, I'd like for you to meet my daughter, Amber. Amber, wave to everybody." He touched her on the shoulder and encouraged her to stand and wave to the other kids. "After I told her what great kids you guys are and what a great trip we had planned, she wanted to come, too."

Sabrina heard the teen girls muttering behind her after his introduction. "Well, ain't that something," Charmaine whispered to her friend, Tawanda. "Mr. Nate got a white daughter. Who would have thought him of all people was into white women?"

Tawanda grunted. "Why is it that lately we see more and more of the good brothers crossing over?" she asked her friend in a hushed tone. "I was sure he was for real, down with sisters."

"Me too," Charmaine said. "He's always going on about black pride. And to think I liked the way he was making the guys respect us and telling them to treasure us because we are their sisters. We are pearls to be treasured," she added sarcastically.

"And all the while, he's kickin' it with white honeys." Tawanda popped her bubble gum loudly and indignantly. "This black-white thing is spreading in Hunter's Creek. The white girls are all over our athletes and the other good-looking ones. If this thing keeps up, we won't have any men for ourselves and we might not even be able to get married. You hear what I'm saying."

"It's getting messed up for sisters," Charmaine agreed somberly as though she were twenty-five instead of a teen. "I hate to see guys passing over us to get with these white women. You see them out and they act like they've won some kind of prize."

"Doesn't it make you sick?" Tawanda added with a disgusted sneer.

"Mr. Nate and Miss Lewis have something going on," Charmaine said in a low, confidential tone that Sabrina could still hear.

"I know," Tawanda said. "I've seen him watching her like she was a chocolate nut sundae with a cherry on top." She giggled.

"Maybe he's had his wake-up call and is coming back home-to us 'Black Pearls'. You know what I mean. Miss Lewis is bad. Fine. She's got her own money and she dresses, too," Charmaine said. "She has what it takes to turn a man around."

"She's cool, too. What does she need a man for? She buys whatever she wants. I wonder what it's like to have it like that. She's about the only sister I know like that." Tawanda popped her gum again. "My mom keeps preaching to me about staying in school, so I can have it like Miss Lewis. My mom says she wants me to have it better than her. Since she and my old man couldn't get along, she's raising us by herself. She has to work hard and then beg my dad to keep up his child support payments for us so we can eat."

"All women need a man, whether they're rich or broke. And you know why, Tawanda," Charmaine said.

The girls' conversation grew soft and full of wicked laughter.

Sabrina figured they were talking about sex. Their attitude wasn't surprising. No matter what age black females were, they seemed to feel betrayed by black men who crossed over. Sabrina bore no contempt for white women. However, she was disappointed by black men who overlooked the beauty and strength of the African-American woman. Times were changing, Sabrina knew. More interracial dating and marriages were occurring every day, whether people liked it or not. Children were being born from these relationships. And Sabrina truly believed with everything in her that these children must not be treated spitefully by black people or white people who opposed interracial relationships.

Nathan took a seat beside Sabrina. "Sorry I had to ask you

to come out of your way this morning. But I knew I could count on you to have this group pulled together by the time I got here." He beamed at her as the driver started the bus to get on their way to the museum. "Amber didn't want to spend a Saturday home with her mom, who wasn't interested in doing anything but reading and relaxing. I told her to come along with us and to be with me. It's good for her to get a taste of her culture, her people. It's something that Caroline has over-looked." He ended his conversation abruptly, snapping his head toward the back of the bus where there was too much noise. Glaring at the horseplay that was taking place, he bolt-ed from his seat to investigate.

Her people, Sabrina thought cynically. She studied Amber as she leaned over the arm of her seat on the school bus, watch-ing her father. Amber Atkins was being raised as a white girl. She had been around white people all her life. Sabrina figured that since Nathan and Caroline were divorced, it was even eas-ier for Caroline not to bother with the fact that Amber had black blood in her veins. This kind of narrow-minded behav-ior exhibited by Caroline was one more reason for Sabrina to censure Nathan's ex.

Returning to his seat beside Sabrina, Nathan shot a warn-ing look to the back of the bus where the rowdy scene had occurred. "We've got to keep our eyes on those two boys. I can't have them making the Hubbard Center look bad, or let people think black folks are uncouth. I'd like to have the option of returning early if the kids misbehave."

"I don't believe they will act out. I've promised them a trip to the pizza parlor. My treat," Sabrina admitted. "They near-ly drove me crazy while we waited for you to show up."

Nathan laughed. "You bribed those rascals. I suppose they'll be on their best behavior for that meal." Nathan grabbed Sabrina's hand and squeezed it. He leaned toward her. "How about us getting together later?" He spoke softly. "You and I need..."

"Nathan, please. Not here," she chided him. "I'm more concerned with getting the kids through this trip. And you should keep your mind on your daughter, since you chose to bring her along." Sabrina turned her attention from him to the sights outside the window. She felt Nathan studying her.

He cleared his throat and shifted restlessly in his seat. "Amber wants me," he said, accepting Sabrina's cold shoulder. He moved to sit beside Amber.

Unconsciously, Sabrina's brow furrowed. She wanted Nathan, but she didn't want to be entangled with his family. It annoyed her that every time Nathan wanted to get together with her in the past few days there was one more thing that he had to do for or with Caroline or Amber. How in the world could he expect Sabrina to be blissful with him, when he had such responsibilities clinging to him? Sabrina grew angry when she thought of how wonderful her and Nathan's relationship could have been about this time, without all the drama and the conflicts they had had. The first few months of any relationship were usually wonderful, she thought, feeling full of resentment. Sabrina glanced to the front of the bus where Nathan was talking softly and smiling into his little girl's face. The sight secretly aroused her fear, the insecurity she felt about involving herself with Nathan. She had given too much of herself too soon. And now she had to deal with her conflicting emotions with him. To keep from being waylaid by heartache, she was going to have to decide whether to open her heart or to just walk away from him for good.

Nathan glanced over his shoulder and caught Sabrina watching him. He gave her an irresistibly devastating grin.

Sabrina was charmed by his attempt. But she didn't let him know. Why did it have to be so complicated? She quickly shifted her attention back out the window and sighed to quell the betrayal of her heart, which tripped with emotion for the man.

Arriving at the Childress Museum, Sabrina and Nathan had to split up in order to keep up with the thirty young people. Because two of the boys chose to do some roughhousing in the museum, Nathan left Amber in Sabrina's care so he could keep a watchful eye on them.

Touring the Black American History Exhibit, Amber constantly wandered away from Sabrina. She touched the delicate displays of the prototypes of the inventions of a shoe-making machine and the first stoplight. Much to Sabrina's chagrin, Amber insisted on sliding back and forth on the shiny marble floors. Finally Sabrina seized the errant child's hand to encourage her to check her conduct. Amber snatched away from Sabrina's grip and gave her a petulant look as if to say: *you can't tell me what to do.* She trotted off to look at some fabulous storytelling—like quilts done by folk artists during slavery times, and she annoyed Sabrina by fingering the designs as though they had come from a toy store. Sabrina sighed in exasperation and followed her.

"Amber, stop it," Sabrina warned, taking her hand again. "I want you here with me until your father returns."

Amber began to whine. "Let go. I'm not a baby!" Her tantrum got the attention of other museum patrons, who were quietly viewing and strolling through the spacious building.

Sabrina grabbed Amber by the hand once more and held on tightly. "Behave yourself. I have more people to think about than just you." She bent and looked Nathan's daughter eye-to-eye to let her know that she meant business.

Amber pouted, but calmed down enough for Sabrina to catch up with the girls she'd left on their own to check out the displays.

Nathan and the others didn't catch up to Sabrina's group until they were studying pictures from the contributions and lives of famous African-American Women. Amber rushed away from Sabrina's side to her father.

"Hey, sweetheart." He smiled at Amber as if he had been gone all day instead of thirty minutes. "The guys were fascinated by the inventors," he told Sabrina. "They were surprised and impressed that such things as the stoplight, machines that stitched shoes, and even the filament in the first light bulb were the ideas of black men," Nathan said. "This was really a great idea, Sabrina. This will stick with a lot of them. And I'm sure it will fuel some of their dreams."

"I hope it does. I fell in love with this exhibit the moment I saw it. I knew the kids had to see this." Sabrina watched as Amber leaned against her father's long leg.

Amber wrinkled her face at Sabrina as though she dared her to say anything in front of her daddy. Sabrina didn't react. She shifted her attention away from Amber. She was thankful that Nathan had shown up. She had had enough of the spoiled girl. She watched Amber wander away from her dad and over to Charmaine and Tawanda, who had beckoned her to them. After overhearing the girls' conversation on the bus, Sabrina knew the girls from the Center were anxious to question Amber about her personal life. There was plenty of curiosity from the girls concerning Amber's sudden appearance in town and her white mother. She knew that Charmaine and Tawanda would keep the child occupied while she and Nathan enjoyed this portion of the tour.

Nathan studied a picture of an impressive woman with a fancy hat decorated with a feather, and smiled. "Madame C. J. Walker. The first Negro Woman to become a millionaire in the United States," he read. "Hey, Sabrina, she made her money from hair products and beauty salons."

"She influenced me." Sabrina stared at the picture of the impeccably dressed woman and smiled with admiration. "Her background is similar to mine. She had no one and no money, as I did. Her parents died when she was a young girl, leaving her in the care of an older married sister who couldn't afford to care for her. But she worked hard and persevered. I read about her in school. I figured that if she did it back in the early 1900s, when times were much more repressive for blacks and women, I could be as successful as she. I merely focused on my dream and worked hard to realize it. That's why it's so important for us to know our contributions. Our people are such an inspiration."

Nathan nodded his approval. "You're right. You have two hair salons, a nail salon and that glamour photography studio that's really taking off in town. Quite a success story for someone your age." He smiled at her. "You're a perfect role model for these kids, just like this Madame Walker was to you."

"Oh, I'm a long way from being perfect, but I'm working on it." Sabrina laughed. Thrilled by the positive interest the kids had for the exhibit at the museum, Sabrina lowered her defenses against Nathan in spite of the bad beginning of their day at his house. She liked the way he looked at her with admiration. It was refreshing to have a man more impressed with your accomplishments than with the shape of your body or the wiggle of your behind, she thought. Ever since Nathan's family had come to town, he and Sabrina had wasted their time and energy quibbling on the phone instead of working on the relationship they had begun to get on the right track before Caroline and Amber blew into town.

"I'm working on my weaknesses, too." His expression of admiration changed to desire. "You and I are going to have to make time for a special evening," he suggested. "This is still February and the next holiday isn't until April. Easter." He chuckled. "We've been holiday lovers." He moved closer to Sabrina and glanced around to see who was near, then he stole a brief, tender kiss from her. "I've been wanting to do that all day."

Sabrina felt radiant and her pulse raced. "Nathan, behave yourself," she reprimanded him with a smile. "Don't give these kids fuel for gossip. We're supposed to be the chaperones."

"Okay, I'll control myself for now. But you can't keep me from thinking about where I'd really like to be with you and what I'd like to be doing." He stared deeply into her eyes, conveying his passion for her.

"Daddy, I'm ready to go," Amber whined, tugging on her father's hand.

Sabrina and Nathan jumped. Amber's grating voice had ended the cozy moment. Nathan dropped down to be eye-level with his daughter. "We'll be ready to leave soon."

Amber threw her arms around her daddy's neck. "Can I call Mommy? We need to call her to see what she's doing."

She stared at Sabrina suspiciously.

"Amber, we'll be going home in a little while." He disentangled the child's arms and stood up.

"I'm thirsty. I want some water," Amber said petulantly, taking his hand.

Nathan sighed. "Come on. Let's find a fountain." He grinned apologetically at Sabrina and walked toward the area where there was a fountain. As they left, Amber looked back over her shoulder at Sabrina and gave her a mean look. Sabrina didn't respond to Amber's behavior. She could imagine that it was difficult for the child to see that her father wanted someone other than her mother.

Amber was shrewd enough to see what was going on between Nathan and her, Sabrina thought. She bet that while Amber was staying with her father she was doing her best to get her parents to make up. Amber probably dreamed of them being one happy family.

In the two times that Sabrina had seen the little girl she had made it clear that she didn't want to be friends with Sabrina. Something Sabrina would have to learn to ignore for now. But if Sabrina and Nathan got closer, she knew that she and Amber were going to have to learn to overcome the rivalry they felt for Nathan's attentions. Sabrina didn't want to be one of those wicked women who sought to make the child a villain to her own father.

In the next couple of weeks, Nathan and Sabrina made an effort to talk and to iron out their differences. The result led to a couple of romantic evenings at her house that renewed her confidence in him and the promise of a healthy relationship.

When Nathan was with Sabrina at her house, they didn't bring up the names of Amber or Caroline. They created their own private world. A paradise of love, with long nights of erotic delights. The delicate flower of her affection blossomed anew. If only they could stay tucked away in her house and away from the realities of his daughter and the ex that he had to contend with, she thought wistfully. There was nothing she wanted more than to become the single most important person in Nathan's life. She knew that this was impossible. Yet every time she was in his arms and making love to him, she wished that it could be a probability.

When Nathan asked Sabrina to do a photo shoot of Amber and himself, she couldn't refuse him. She figured this would be a good chance for her to work at winning Amber over, now that she and Nathan were at peace with each other. Even though her business catered to women, she relented and agreed to do a father-daughter shooting only for him. He had related to her that he wanted to have something special to remind him of Amber. They had never had a family portrait made, he admitted to Sabrina. And during that time he was separated from Amber, he had decided the first chance he had he would have a picture made of the two of them. He wanted one for himself and one for his daughter. That way she could be reminded of his love for her.

Nathan appeared at Sabrina's studio dressed in a tailored gray suit, and Amber wore a yellow dress that made her look like an angel. Thankfully, they had come without Caroline hovering over them.

Sabrina touched up Amber's face lightly with a little powder and some lipstick to bring out her features. She combed and fluffed Amber's thick hair so it would look perfect in the picture.

When Camille set Nathan and Amber before her camera, Sabrina stood in the background to observe them being photographed.

On one pose, Amber stood beside her father, who sat. She had her arm around his shoulder. Another pose was taken with her sitting in front of Nathan. They smiled as though they had the most serene life in the world. Another pose was taken of them beaming at each other and giggling. That particular pose was Amber's idea. Camille took other poses of the two. And Amber loved every minute of the attention she got from her father.

Sabrina couldn't help but admire their relationship. The father-daughter bond was strange to her. She hadn't known her own father. Nathan's mouth curved into a smile each time his daughter looked at him. Though Amber grew restless and playful during the session, he never became impatient.

When Camille was done, Nathan hugged his daughter and kissed her on the top of her head.

Sabrina left the room to answer the telephone. It was Caroline.

"Is my husband..." Caroline laughed. "Oh, silly me. Uh, I mean are Nathan and Amber still there?" she asked.

"Yes, they are," Sabrina said curtly. "Would you like to speak with Nathan?" she asked, disliking Caroline's arrogant tone.

"Please, dear."

Sabrina wanted to hang up on the woman.

Nathan came out of the back with Amber trailing behind him and giggling over a shared joke.

"It's Caroline." Sabrina handed him the portable phone. It took everything in her to hide the irritation that Caroline's sarcasm always invoked in her. She hurried over to her make-up station and busied herself, clearing away the things she had used. Nathan stood near Sabrina.

"Yes, we're all done," Nathan said. "I was planning on taking Amber for something to eat." He walked away from Sabrina and stood in front of Romantic Poses' picture window, staring outside while he listened to Caroline.

Amber wandered up to Sabrina and gave her a more friendly smile than she ever had. Had it been because she had made her look pretty for her pictures? Sabrina wondered. Had she and the little girl finally found grounds not to be rivals?

Sabrina motioned the child to a chair. "How about taking a seat to let me remove that make-up?"

"Can I keep it on, Sabrina?" Amber asked, giving her a pleading look. She folded her arms on top of her head.

"But your father is taking you out. I only put the lipstick and powder on you to make your pictures look nicer," Sabrina explained. She bent down to look Amber in the eyes. "Little girls aren't suppose to wear make-up like this all the time."

"But I like it. I want to keep it on." Amber skipped over to where her father stood, still talking to her mother. She narrowed her eyes at Sabrina as though she dared her to try to remove the make-up.

Brat, Sabrina thought. So much for her hope of friendship with Amber. She had her father wrapped around her little finger. From what Sabrina had observed of Amber's behavior, Caroline hadn't disciplined her much. Amber had her way far too much and she could really be obnoxious when she wanted to be.

Amber tugged on Nathan's arm. "Let me talk to Mommy."

Nathan muttered a few words, then handed the phone to Amber. When he turned to face Sabrina, she noticed that his brow was furrowed.

"Those pictures are going to be fabulous," Sabrina said, hoping he wouldn't speak about Caroline to her.

"That young lady, Camille, seems to know what she's doing. I can't wait to see the proofs." Nathan walked up to Sabrina and tenderly touched her on the shoulder.

Sabrina moved away from him. She didn't like displaying affection in front of his daughter. And with Caroline on the phone, it made her feel doubly uncomfortable. She didn't want Amber relating their actions to Caroline. It was none of Caroline's business what happened between her and Nathan. "Amber won't let me take that make-up off."

"I figured that was going to happen. I saw the way her eyes lit up when you pulled out those brushes and that lipstick and went to work on her." He glanced at his daughter, who knelt on a chair, talking on the phone to her mother. "She has to get out of that make-up. I was planning on taking her out to get something to eat. I wanted to make the day special for us."

"That's nice. I'm sure she'll never forget today. You are a good father." Sabrina smiled at him.

"It's a special job. I regret that she has been away from me so long. There's so much I've missed. I've really enjoyed having her around."

"I can imagine," Sabrina agreed. On the inside, she disagreed with him. But who was she to stand between him and the love of his daughter? The only thing she truly resented was the interference in their personal lives.

Amber rushed over to the counter and set the phone aside. She hopped into Sabrina's chair. "You can take the make-up off. Mommy told me that since we were going to dinner I couldn't wear this stuff. It would make me look silly, she said."

"And she is right," Sabrina said. She resented doing what she had wanted to do in the first place. Now she felt as if she was following Caroline's orders. She proceeded to use her special creams to remove the make-up from the child's face. Inside she was feeling envious. They were going out to dinner together like one big happy family. And it was that bond of Amber that Caroline had with Nathan that posed a threat to Sabrina and the relationship she was attempting to have with him. No matter how much he tried to convince Sabrina that all the deep feelings he had had for his ex had faded, she still felt as though Amber was capable of bringing her parents back together again. Anything involving Amber could bring them together, Sabrina thought with dread.

"Caroline has been out shopping," Nathan said. "She hasn't eaten and asked to join us."

Sabrina said nothing as she carefully put the finishing touches on cleaning the little girl's face. "There you go, Miss Amber."

Amber hopped down from the chair. "I have to use the bathroom." She looked up at her father.

"It's straight to the back," Sabrina instructed, pointing out the room.

Once Amber trotted off to the restroom, Nathan sidled up

beside Sabrina. "Caroline insisted upon being with Amber and me. She's jealous of how close Amber and I have gotten in the short time they have been back."

"Short time? Nathan, they've been at your house for almost a month. I have a feeling that Caroline isn't planning on going anywhere," she said sardonically. She had been waiting for just the right time to voice her opinion.

"Don't worry. She won't be living with me. She's trying to find a job. She has been going on interviews."

"Interviews? She's going to live in Hunter's Creek?" Sabrina scowled at Nathan.

"Well, yes. She thought it would be good for her to live in the area. That way she and I could share custody of Amber. She admits that being a single parent is hard for her. Amber can be a handful. Uh...we enrolled Amber in school the other day."

"Oh, I see," Sabrina said. She was hurt that he hadn't mentioned this to her before now. But her feelings shouldn't have been bruised. After all, when they were together, they had decided to only talk of things concerning them and their relationship. Her ignorance regarding Caroline and Amber had been blissful when she was alone and lost in rapture with him. "Is Caroline going to continue to live with you?" Sabrina snapped. The news of the school business didn't sit well with her at all. Why had he kept something like that from her?

"Oh, no. She's going to get a place of her own as soon as she can get a job," he said, trying to reassure her.

Amber burst back into the room. "I'm ready, Daddy," she declared, slipping her hand into his.

"Okay, let's go, sweetheart." He leaned over and kissed Sabrina on the lips. "I'll call you later." He strolled out of Romantic Poses with his daughter strutting beside him.

Sabrina sat in the chair where Amber had sat only moments ago. She felt as if she wanted to scream. Learning that Amber had been enrolled in school only confirmed Sabrina's suspicions that Caroline was intending to work her way back into Nathan's life.

Sabrina heaved a sigh of resignation and went into the dressing room to prepare the outfits and accessories for her next appointment. She couldn't let herself worry over something that was spinning out of control. She heard someone enter the salon. Setting aside the costume jewelry to be used, she rushed to the reception area. She was surprised to find Malcolm Knight.

"Sabrina, how are you?" He gave her a dazzling smile.

After all she had been through, he was the last person that Sabrina wanted to see.

Chapter Eight

Malcolm strolled over to Sabrina. "Oh, 'Brina, don't look at me that way. I'm not here to harm you or to start trouble this time. Nor am I looking for rent money like I used to. For your interest, I got rid of that place. The rent got a little too steep." A smile magnified his handsome features. "I come in peace. In these last few weeks, a lot has changed for the better for me. I'd hoped you'd be interested to know what's up with me."

"I'm happy for you," Sabrina deadpanned. "I don't have time for any foolishness or lies." She folded her arms at her waist and crimped her mouth with annoyance.

"Neither do I." Malcolm kept his distance, as though he didn't want to alarm her in any way. He unzipped his short jacket, placed his hands in the pockets of his jeans and jingled the loose change there. He was calmer, more full of confidence than the last time she had seen him. "I have some good news I'd like to share with you." His chestnut complexion radiated cheer.

"Malcolm, I'm not interested in you or your news." She sauntered to the other side of the room where she spotted the purse that belonged to Amber. She pretended not to be interested in Malcolm or the news he wanted to share. Her interest would only encourage a friendship she wasn't ready to accept. She picked up the purse and walked past Malcolm to put it behind the counter. She'd give Nathan a call later to tell him that his daughter had left it.

"I don't believe you." His intense gaze followed her. "You should care. We were together long enough for you to want to

112

know what's going on with me whether it's good or bad. You pretend you're the tough lady you seem to be. But I've seen you with your defenses down. That little girl in you. I loved that side just as much as I did the professional businesswoman side you present to the public." He gave her a knowing grin. "I care about you. I still make it my business to find out about you from whomever I can. I still care and I always will, lady." He stared at her with a wistful yearning. "You've invested enough money and interest in me for me to care. I owe you more than money. If it hadn't been for you, I wouldn't be where I am."

"You're mighty dramatic today. What brings all of this on?" She regarded him with a lofty expression. "I have too many important things on my mind to care what you do or where you go."

Malcolm's dark eyes locked into hers. He smiled wryly. "When you're like this, you're sexy. Remember how turned on I used to get when we argued?" His seductive gaze grazed her shapely body from head to toe. "Hmm...you can be quite a pistol. Yes, you can!" His eyes glimmered as though he was having lustful flashbacks.

A young girl in her mid-teens entered the shop, interrupting Malcolm's trip down memory lane. The African-American girl had come to pick up the Romantic Poses she had taken for her sixteenth birthday. As Sabrina pulled her pictures from the long, low file cabinet and laid them out, she too remembered the heated arguments she and Malcolm had had. And, yes, they had often turned into heated, passionate trysts that made them set aside their differences.

"These are gorgeous, Yolanda. Your personality really shines through," Sabrina told the young girl, spreading out the pictures. She glanced at Malcolm; he had taken a seat and was watching her seductively.

The young, cinnamon-complexioned girl studied the soft, sophisticated pictures of herself. Her eyes glowed with pride and awe. "Miss Lewis, you made me look beautiful!"

"You are beautiful, Yolanda. I hope your parents will be as

pleased as you are." Sabrina slid the photos into her specially designed folder, placed them in a plastic bag and handed them to her young customer. "Here you are. Be sure to spread the word to your friends."

"Oh, I will," the young lady enthused. She hustled out of the shop, clutching her pictures as though they were a treasure.

"Quite a set-up." Malcolm eased out of his seat and ambled over to the counter. "I suppose this place—along with those beauty salons and the nail salon in the mall—has been worth the break-up of our relationship." His tone dripped with sarcasm.

Sabrina shot him a no-nonsense glance. "Don't start with me. If it wasn't for the time I put into this business and my other investments, I wouldn't have been able to help you handle your expenses in New York."

"Ouch! You didn't have to go there." He leaned on the counter until she could smell the soft, clean fragrance of his cologne. He touched her face and smiled.

Pursing her lips, Sabrina jerked away from him.

"I appreciate everything you've done for me," he said. "I promise to pay back every dollar you spent on me. I kept my records." He brushed his neatly trimmed moustache. "I came here to see you and to let you know that your investment in me has finally kicked in. I have an agent and the job offers are pouring in for me."

In spite of herself, Sabrina's eyes brightened with interest. "Congratulations! Someone has finally recognized your talent." She couldn't help but feel happy for him. No one knew better than she how much he wanted a career in show business . "What kind of jobs are we talking about here?" She relaxed and leaned on the counter near him.

"I knew you'd be interested," he told her, clearly pleased he had melted her cool attitude. "I have gotten a bit part in an upcoming movie. A comedy with this new young black director. It's only a few lines. But the character I play is really wild and should draw a lot of attention. Then I'm scheduled to do a pilot for a situation comedy. And best of all, I'm going on tour with the super pop diva, Tamisha. She caught my act in New York and had her agent sign me to be the warm-up act for her upcoming summer tour. Can you believe my luck?"

"Tamisha is fabulous. Everyone loves her. I have all of her CDs. I'm really impressed," Sabrina said. She honestly meant the compliment. "You should be ecstatic that your dream is becoming a reality."

He tilted his head slightly and gazed at her with those wonderful, dark eyes of his. "I am happy. But it would be even more sweet if I had you to share all this with me. You're the only person who knows what I've been through to get this far."

Sabrina ran her hand through her hair, lost in thought. Yes, all of this could have been reason to celebrate a few months ago. There had been a time when she wanted nothing more than to see her man, Malcolm, hit the big time. But now she could only share his joy as a casual acquaintance would. Nothing more. Since she had discovered him cheating, she wanted no part of his life, no matter how successful he became. He had lost her trust. As far as she was concerned, without trust there could be no love, no relationship.

"You've worked hard. You deserve your happiness," she said softly. She gave him a modest smile. "Enjoy it."

"I'll do my best." Malcolm gave Sabrina a sad, regretful look. It was too late to convince her that he really loved her for whom she was, not just for her money. "Just think, I could have had it all with you at my side. I was a fool to allow other women to turn me around and to forget the one person who truly cared about me. You have to believe me when I say that no other woman has meant more to me than you have. I might not have been 'Mr. Perfect.' But I'm a man with needs that you didn't have time to fulfill." His voice took on an edge of blame. "That's why I was such an easy mark to other women—"

"Okay." Sabrina cut him off. She was irked that he tried to turn his infidelity into her fault. "We don't have to go down that road anymore. What we had is done and over. You're doing okay and I am most certainly moving on with my life and doing what I love, too." The steam of his self-righteous accusation poured out of him like hot air from a balloon.

She sauntered from behind the counter to meet the mail-man who had entered Romantic Poses. She greeted the man with a friendly smile and accepted the letters and packages he gave her. She walked to the counter near Malcolm and laid down the mail, then proceeded to sift through the day's parcels and letters.

Malcolm sidled closer. He placed his arm around her waist and smiled. "I came here to bring you something."

That dazzling smile of his was what usually won her over to him. It wasn't working this time. The magic was gone. Her heart was hardened to all his charms. She gave him a skepti-cal look. "I hope you didn't waste your money on a gift for me. There's nothing I want from you."

He reached inside his jacket pocket, pulled out a white envelope and handed it to her. "My first payment."

Ripping open the envelope, Sabrina pulled out a check for five thousand dollars. She gasped in surprise.

"Once I get to working, I'll be able to make another pay-ment to clear my debt to you. I'm determined to give you back all the money you spent on me. When you were wearing my ring, I considered the money you spent an investment in our future. You know, the husband and wife thing we'd dreamed of."

"I have to respect you for doing the right thing by me." Sabrina stuffed the check back in the envelope. She hadn't expected to see a dime of the money she'd given him. She had written the deal off as a bad experience where she had allowed a man to use her. Because she had cared about him, she had wanted to help him.

Malcolm covered her hand with his. "I'd give anything to turn back the hands of time. I wish I could erase that unpleas-ant sight from your mind of me with that other woman. Have you forget and forgive me and make me your man again," he said apologetically. He leaned over and kissed her face.

His voice and words would have been hypnotic if she still

cared, she told herself. The only emotion she could elicit was sympathy for him for destroying what they had shared. Sabrina moved away from him. She held up the check. "I appreciate this. And your apology means a lot. It's more than I expected." She wouldn't look him in the eyes. She didn't want to encourage him with what he might think he saw in her eyes or expression.

Malcolm gave a resigned shrug. "I suppose I should leave. Knowing you, you have something more important you'd rather be doing than chatting with your ex-lover, right?"

"I'm a businesswoman. I'll always be one." She managed a forced smile.

"But you're a woman, too. You're an exciting and passionate woman who needs more than several businesses and a fat bank account to satisfy you."

Sabrina swung her gaze to meet his and glared at him. His comment insulted her. Then she looked at her watch. "I appreciate you coming by, but I still have a long day ahead of me," she said, dismissing him and any further personal comments he might make.

"Yeah. Sure." He sighed with resignation. "How about a hug for good luck? I don't know when I'll be back in Hunter's Creek." He held open his arms to her.

Reluctantly, Sabrina returned his embrace. Once she was in his arms, he held her and kissed the side of her face. "I was such a fool." He held her away so that he could look into her eyes. "Maybe one day you and I will find that magic again. One day you can forgive me." He grinned and hugged her again. "Sabrina, Sabrina. My angel."

"Good luck to you, Malcolm." Sabrina responded to his affection and embraced him to say good-bye. For good, she hoped.

Suddenly, the front door opened and Nathan walked in. "Oh, excuse me," he said. "I...uh...did Amber leave her pocketbook here?" His eyes danced with jealousy at the two, embracing.

Sabrina grew warm with embarrassment. She laughed

nervously. "I have it right here." She released Malcolm and went to the reception desk where she had placed Amber's purse.

In that instant, she sized up the two men. Malcolm stood at her picture window with his hands behind his back, staring at the passing traffic. She had nearly married him. There had been no great love for him, the kind she knew she was supposed to have. But there had been enough sexual passion and compatibility between them to build a marriage, she had figured. She had been in her late twenties and she had admired his ambition and his professional desire. At that time she believed they were perfectly suited for one another. He had come from the same blue-collar neighborhood she had. And many of the boys from the neighborhood were still doing the same things they had done as kids—nothing but hanging around, getting in trouble. She and Malcolm had been with the group of kids who learned a vocation or went to college. Though Malcolm was beginning to see his hard work come to fruition, Sabrina knew he wasn't the man for her. Thinking over their relationship, Sabrina could now see how Malcolm was the kind of man who used love and sex for recreational purposes. Comforts to entertain and please him when they suited him best. And toward the end of their romance, she had had the feeling at times that he resented her success and her being the one who controlled their relationship with her money. Malcolm needed the kind of woman who would support his career and idolize him. Sabrina knew that she would be miserable living that kind of life after being independent and business-minded for so long

Malcolm turned and winked at Sabrina. Clearly an attempt to woo her back. She was unfazed. She wished Malcolm would vanish. He had made his apologies and given her a partial payment on the money. And she had wished him well. As far as she was concerned, it was over between them.

Nathan, on the other hand, was unlike any man she had known before. He had shown her that real love was tender and caring. He was strong and confident and intelligent. She had learned that he had taken several courses toward a law degree. He hoped to become a criminal lawyer soon and one day even a judge. As a police officer who had worked in a large city and then in Hunter's Creek, he had seen far too many brothers and other black people get shafted by the system. He wanted to be the kind of lawyer who could make a difference and hopefully turn someone's life around. Sabrina admired him for his ideals. There was no doubt in her mind that he would make a great lawyer and a great judge, too, if he so desired.

Though Sabrina was attracted to Nathan and thought the world of him, she was scared to open her heart completely. Nathan had too much baggage for her to intertwine her life with his just yet. He had an ex-wife who depended upon him as though they were still married. And then there was his obnoxious daughter, Amber, who made it clear she didn't like Sabrina. Their new relationship, which had taken off like a skyrocket, was now on shaky ground. Sabrina didn't know how much more she could take of sharing Nathan. She wanted to be more open-minded, for Nathan's sake. But her anxiety and fears kept getting in the way.

Nathan didn't acknowledge Malcolm. He ignored him. He stood tall with a somber expression. Sabrina's heart turned over at the sight of Nathan and the sullen attitude he showed toward her ex. It was definitely a validation of his strong affections for her. She knew he didn't want Malcolm to hurt her any more than he already had. Nathan was the kind of man she needed. He had principles and sensitivity. It was obvious that he cared about all women and viewed them as more than just sex objects. In fact, he had made it clear he admired her independence and her bright mind. He wasn't threatened by who she was or who she wanted to be.

"Here you are," Sabrina said, picking up Amber's pocketbook. "A lady needs her purse." She forced a laugh. "You enjoy your dinner."

Nathan accepted the purse, but held on to her hand. "What is he doing here?" he asked in a low, confidential tone.

"It's okay. We're finishing off old business. He doesn't

have enough excuses like Caroline does to keep her in your life."

Nathan flinched from her accusation. His jawline flexed in aggravation. Unexpected triumph flooded through Sabrina. She had held in her true feelings too long.

Nathan's eyes grew cold. "I have to go. Have fun with the clown." He tilted his head in a curt nod and marched out the door.

The moment that Nathan was gone, Sabrina hated herself for the comment she had made. But she hated the insecurity she experienced from Caroline even more. She wondered if her feelings of resentment would be the same had Caroline been a black woman.

Malcolm touched Sabrina on the shoulder. She jumped and shot him an impatient look. She'd forgotten all about him.

He held her by the elbow. "I didn't mean to frighten you. You look as though you could use a friend to talk to. Let's go get some coffee and..."

She held up her hand to dismiss the idea. "I'm fine. I just need to be alone."

He shrugged and nodded with understanding. "Sure. Well, I'm leaving. You take care." He leaned in for another kiss.

Sabrina turned her head aside. "Good-bye, Malcolm."

"Yeah. Sure." Then he too disappeared from Romantic Poses.

Sabrina's throat ached with despair. Forget both of them, she thought. She hustled into her back room to preview the proofs that Camille had left for her. As usual, her businesses were the only constants in her life. She had no luck with men and making relationships work. But she had become quite proficient in knowing exactly how to make her work her lover.

Still, her spirits plummeted. Her heart wasn't convinced that she could live without the love of a man. And for the moment, the one she wanted was inaccessible to her. He was Nathan Atkins. Her vision grew blurry with tears while she studied the proofs. She set them aside and gave in to her tears of sadness.

Chapter Nine

The moment Sabrina opened the door of the Soul Food Inn, the aroma of barbecued ribs, chicken, and desserts flavored with vanilla tickled her nose. Her stomach roiled in hunger. It was past noon, and she had only had a glass of juice with a dry piece of toast at six o'clock that morning.

"There's my princess!" Grace sang out. She stood at the cash register, checking out the take-out customers.

The people who crowded the restaurant turned to look at Sabrina; she was dressed in a navy blue suit with a yellow blouse. She wore her raven-colored hair combed behind her ears to reveal her diamond-studded earrings. They'd been a gift to herself after her first successful year of business at the Lovely Nails Boutique in the mall. Sabrina made her way to the back of the restaurant, the way she had done since she was in school and came to meet her mother.

Today, March sixth, was her mother's birthday. Sabrina had come to bring her mother her gift. She hadn't been able to catch up with her at home. The two of them had no idea what the other's schedule was because of their lack of communication. Sabrina had grown used to not being able to pin her mother down in order to spend time with her. In the past, it had hurt that her mother didn't care enough to want to spend time with her, but as the years passed she had come to terms with their estrangement. She respected Grace. But it was too late for them to have a traditional mother-daughter thing.

Grace made her way slowly through the crowd of customers. Sabrina studied how personable she was with everyone. A broad smile, a pat on the back, or a whisper in the ear that elicited laughter. Grace knew how to talk to everyone but Sabrina. She and her mother couldn't be around each other for more than a few hours at a time. They'd either grow restless or begin to have words over something petty and ridiculous.

"Baby, I told Clara to bring you some of the ribs, a scoop of macaroni and cheese, some of those collards and some cornbread. I bet you can't remember the last time you had a good solid meal."

"Hmm...that sounds delicious," Sabrina said in a reluctant tone. Grace always wanted to feed her. It was the only sign of nurturing her mother could comfortably show.

"I tried to call you this morning for your birthday, but I guess you were sound asleep," Sabrina said. She reached into her purse and pulled out a small, rose-colored, wrapped package.

"I didn't stay at home last night. Dennis and I started celebrating early." Grace winked. "I couldn't take the day off. You know, Mr. Jenkins, the boss, is still in the hospital, getting over his hip surgery. I promised to run things 'til he got better. He knows I'm the only one he can trust with his place."

Sabrina tried not to show her disapproval of her mother sleeping with Dennis. She knew Grace had stopped caring what her daughter thought of her behavior a long time ago. She laid the package in front of her mother. "Happy Birthday, Grace...uh, Mama." Though their relationship wasn't easy, Sabrina loved giving her mother expensive gifts. Even at her age and with her success, she still sought her mother's approval and the crumbs of her love.

"Sweetie, that's so kind of you." Grace beamed. She loved surprises, Sabrina knew. Especially from her daughter.

"How does it feel to be forty-nine?" Sabrina asked, watching her mother rip away the paper. She couldn't wait for her mother's reaction to what she had selected for her.

Seeing how loving and attentive Nathan was with his daughter, Sabrina yearned to build a better relationship with her own mother. Sabrina had always felt all these years that she and her mother weren't a real family. The idea had been fixed in her childhood mind that a real family had both a mother and a father. But now Nathan had shown her that the most important ingredients to a family were love and respect. And in the last few years, Grace had been much better at attempting to do both of those things the best she could. Sabrina had to respect her for the effort.

"Shh...don't tell everyone in the place my age. Some of these people think I'm your big sister." Grace laughed robustly, then gasped when she saw the gray jewelry box. She opened the lid and let out a roar of delight that caught everyone's attention in the Soul Food Inn. She bolted from her seat, went to her daughter and gave her a kiss on the cheek that left behind a smudge of her raisin-colored lipstick. "I've been wanting one of these for a long time." She took out the cluster diamond ring, slipped it on her finger and held it up to admire it.

"I'm glad you like it." Sabrina gloried in the moment. She hadn't expected her mother to be so openly affectionate in the restaurant.

Clara, one of the waitresses about her mother's age, appeared and served Sabrina a platter of food. She took Grace's hand to admire the ring. "You're a lucky woman to have such a sweet child. That's beautiful, Sabrina."

"Thanks, Clara." Sabrina smiled at the older woman, took a napkin, placed it in her lap and began eating the soul food, which she allowed herself to eat only on special occasions. She loved it but if she ate the tasty food too often, she knew that she wouldn't continue to be a perfect size nine.

Her mother ate a slice of sweet potato pie and chatted while Sabrina worked her way through the meal. "Your new man was in here the other day," Grace said in a casual tone. "He caused quite a stir among the waitresses. If I hadn't been here, he and his 'guests' might not have gotten served."

"What happened?" Sabrina sipped on her iced tea. She knew her mother was speaking of Caroline and Amber. But she was curious to hear what her mother had to say.

"He was with this white woman and I guess her daughter."

Sabrina shifted her attention outside the window. Grace had met Nathan when Sabrina had brought him to the restaurant a couple of weeks earlier. However, she had never told her mother that Nathan's ex-wife was in town with their daughter, and that the woman happened to be white.

"That was Nathan's ex-wife, Caroline, and their daughter, Amber," Sabrina said matter-of-factly.

"What? You got rid of my Malcolm for a man who likes white women?" Grace eyed her daughter with disbelief.

"Malcolm helped me to make the decision to lose Malcolm. I didn't break-up with Malcolm because of Nathan. I wasn't even interested in Nathan then," Sabrina informed her mother.

"I see her out and about town with that little girl." Grace sniffed in disgust. "She walks around like she is some kind of royalty. Why did she show up? I thought you and he had a little something going on."

Sabrina shrugged. "She brought his daughter to be with him. They'd been estranged for a couple of years. Amber wanted to see her father. That's all I know. That's all I want to know," she said with a perfectly passionless expression on her face.

"You're pissed off about the whole situation. I can tell," Grace said. She lit up a cigarette and took a drag. "Where is the 'queen' living while she's here?"

"Uh...with Nathan." Sabrina smiled to mask her anxiety. She didn't want her mother to get too personal about her least favorite subject.

"What? What kind of stuff is that?" Grace asked vehemently. "You're going to lose this man, too. You don't let another woman live with your man. There's too much temptation. Suppose they get those old feelings going again? And boom! You're out of the picture."

Sabrina rubbed the back of her neck where she felt tension growing. "Nathan has assured me that he has no feelings for his ex. He's only putting her up to be with his daughter. She'll be moving out as soon as she can find a job."

"A job? That one looks like she hasn't worked a day in her life. She is the kind of woman who is used to having a man take care of her." Grace gave her daughter a warning look.

Sabrina couldn't deny what her mother was saying. She definitely agreed with her mother on all the points she had made. But she had decided to trust Nathan. Things had been strained between them because of the situation. But he had gone out of his way to remind her—to convince her-that she was important to him.

"I've enjoyed the meal, Mom. And it was nice chatting with you," she said to dismiss her mother's two-cents opinion of her life. "I'm sure you're not done celebrating."

"Of course not. Dennis got something planned for me with some of our card-playing friends." Grace looked away from Sabrina as if she felt guilty for excluding her. But they both knew her daughter wouldn't have come if she'd invited her. Her bright, beautiful daughter had outgrown her background, her friends, a long time ago. "Thanks so much for this ring, baby." Grace reached out, took Sabrina's hand and stroked it tenderly. "You're something else. You're the kind of woman I wish I could have been," she said softly. Tears glistened in her eyes. "It's your father's misfortune that he never knew you."

At the unexpected mention of her never-spoken-of father, Sabrina's eyes pooled with tears and a sadness filled her heart.

"I wish I had known him," Sabrina admitted softly. "You know, Ma, part of the reason I've worked and struggled so hard to succeed has been with my father in mind. If I was success-ful enough, I thought, he would seek me out, want to know me and be proud to have me as his child," she said. Her voice quivered. She wiped away the tears that had spilled down her face and met under her chin. "Isn't that ridiculous for a woman like me to think that way?" She forced a proud smile through her tears.

"Oh, baby, no, I understand," Grace cooed affectionately, squeezing her hand. At the pain she saw in her child's eyes, her tears fell as well.

Sabrina sniffled and stared fondly at her mother. She covered her hand with hers. Grace's display of kindness and caring during her most vulnerable moment had been priceless. It was unusual for either of them to show their honest feelings with each other. Sabrina was warmed by her mother's love. It was a beautiful feeling, a memory that would hold a sacred place in her heart.

That evening, Sabrina took a long bubble bath. She thought about the visit with her mother and was glad that she had taken the time to see her. She was also filled with excited anticipation, preparing for an evening with Nathan at her place. Two previous dates of theirs had been canceled, because of the inconvenience Caroline had placed on him. Lately, she had developed the habit of driving to the next town to visit old college friends while leaving Amber in Nathan's care. By the time Caroline arrived back at Nathan's the evening would be ruined. Nathan always wound up apologizing and making new plans with Sabrina. This made Sabrina furious. She had had to miss out on plans to eat at a fabulous restaurant, and once had even wasted tickets on a Broadway drama that had come to town.

Nathan had promised Sabrina that the plans she had for tonight of preparing dinner and sharing a night of romance wouldn't be ruined. He had the teenage daughter of one of his co-workers on call, just in case Caroline became thoughtless again.

Sabrina dressed in jeans and a fluffy pink sweater. The food was in the oven warming and the dining room table had been set with her brand new china and silverware, which she had never used.

When the telephone rang, she was going through her CD collection and picking out music to add ambience to an evening of romance that was long overdue.

Sabrina answered the telephone. It was Nathan. "No, Nathan. I can't believe this is happening again," she said the moment she heard the apologetic tone in his voice.

"Take it easy, Sabrina. Hear me out. Caroline had to leave town this afternoon for a family emergency. Her father had a heart attack."

"I'm sorry to hear that. I really am. I know you're going to miss Amber."

"Amber didn't go. She's here with me. I told her mother I'd take good care of her until she could come back." He paused. "Why don't you come here? Amber has been fed and she has had her bath. She'll be asleep soon."

"But what about the wonderful romantic dinner I prepared for you?" Sabrina was frustrated with the thought of yet another spoiled evening.

"Bring it. We can warm it in the oven and then I can get all cozy with you." His voice was low and sexy.

The timbre of his voice sent shivers up her spine. Her body ached with desire. She had been without his tender loving too long to turn down his invitation.

"I'll be there within the hour," she answered in a sultry voice.

"See, I told you Amber would pose no problems. She fell asleep halfway through that video I bought to keep her company," Nathan said as he placed the last dish into the dishwasher.

He moved to the table where Sabrina was wrapping the leftovers from their meal. He couldn't resist touching her for another minute. He stood behind her and locked his arms around her waist. The mere touch of her softly-rounded body caused his latent love to emerge. He nuzzled his face into her soft, fragrant hair and placed a kiss on the back of her neck. He was intoxicated by the lavender scent of her cologne.

Sabrina covered his hands with her own and leaned back to

accept his affection.

Nathan kissed her face and held his cheek next to hers. "We've been away from each other much too long." He emphasized the words with another kiss on her face.

Whirling around to face him, Sabrina rested her hands on his chest and gazed into his eyes, smiling. "I have missed not being with you the way I want." She layered his neck with feathery kisses.

Nathan sighed. He felt a pang of love with the affection that Sabrina offered him. "Tonight, we can make up for lost time. Amber is sound asleep. We can hide away in my bedroom to clear away all of our frustrations." He chuckled, then lowered a hand to her bottom and pulled her against his arousal. A jolt of excitement flowed to his heart as she ground herself slowly upon his bulging passion. He held her chin and set to nibbling her lips gently before covering her sensual mouth with his. He enfolded her in his arms and gave her a slow, thoughtful kiss. His tongue traced the fullness of her lips, then slipped inside her mouth to explore its recesses. He slid his hand under her sweater and was pleased to find that she was braless and that her nipples were pouted with arousal.

Sabrina clung to him, breathing hotly. Her mind grew clouded with lust. She was anxious to be undressed and in bed with him. "What about those satin sheets and scented candles you promised me?" she whispered as he continued to kiss every inch of her face.

"I didn't forget. Everything is all set," he murmured between delicious kisses.

"Hmm...what are we doing in here then?" she asked, looping her arms around his neck.

"Exactly." He whirled her away from him and scooped her off the floor and into his arms.

She giggled with delight. "How gallant of you." She fitted her face against the crook of his neck as he rushed off with her to his bedroom.

He set Sabrina on the floor and locked the bedroom door. While Sabrina disrobed, he lit the six scented candles that sat on the nightstands on both sides of his bed. When that tedious job was completed, he turned out the lights to find Sabrina standing nude and looking radiant in the candlelight. She was a vision.

She gave him an inviting look and turned down the bed. "Get out of those clothes. I'm on fire." She licked a fingertip, touched her hip and made a sizzling noise to tease him. She climbed onto the cool black satin sheets and propped up on the pillows to watch Nathan remove his clothes.

As she watched him strip, her prolonged anticipation was almost unbearable. She saw a heart-rending tenderness in his gaze that convinced her that their encounter was going to be memorable, thrilling. Her eyes raked boldly over his beautiful nude body and lingered a bit longer on his erection, which was firm and ready. There was a tingling in the pit of her stomach when she imagined how wonderful it would feel to have him buried within her.

"Nathan, don't tease me any longer," she said in a sultry voice, settling upon the pillows and parting her legs to entice him.

Nathan came to her and swept her into his arms. He held her against him until she could feel his racing heart against her pounding one. In the glow of the scented candles, Nathan became her angel of love. As his long, strong body covered hers, she felt as though she was drowning in a sea of love. She was ready to accede to anything he might suggest. She grew limp from his hot tongue-kisses and the feel of his warm, magnificent hands touching her here and there to electrify her.

Sliding against the luxurious, silky sheets intensified the pleasure of their lovemaking. As he hovered over her, she felt as though she was in paradise. His lips graced her neck and moved to her breasts with their nipples peaked like rosebuds. He ran his tongue around each point before sucking it ever so gently.

Sabrina moaned and writhed from the heat that settled in her feminine essence. Nathan kissed her between her breasts and made his way down to her tummy where his mouth toyed with her belly-button. He flicked his tongue in and out while he caressed her soft pubic hair. She was wet; she quivered as she felt his strong fingers move up and down the pearl of her feminine essence. Lost in a probing tongue kiss, he slipped his fingers in and out of her love cave, sending her to the edge of ecstasy. Weakened and mesmerized by all she felt, Sabrina uttered a murmur that resembled the purr of a kitten.

Nathan's sexy voice interrupted her erotic delight. "I have to be inside of you. I can't wait any longer." He fitted his body between her thighs and filled her with him. He groaned. His member pulsated inside her as though he was ready to climax. He begged Sabrina not to make a move. He was not ready for this interlude to be over just yet. She held him gently and kissed him in understanding. She slowed her breathing, caressing his face with sighs; it helped her to restrain the passion she was ready to unleash.

Nathan held her and rested his forehead against hers. He proceeded to move slowly within her. Sabrina welcomed his motion and fell into the sweet tempo he had begun. Her flesh grew moist and his felt fevered. She raised her legs and locked them around his hips. She wanted to pull him deeper inside her. She cradled his body and couldn't resist the urge to rock him wildly. Her action sent him into a frenzy. He held her tightly and grunted with each deep thrust he lavished upon her. Soon they fell headlong into the sticky, tangled web of desire that sent waves of golden pleasure washing through Sabrina. They shuddered and moaned until they lay spent in each other's arms.

Just as Nathan rolled off her, the telephone rang. He cursed, snatched the phone off the receiver and grumbled hello. He sat upright in bed and looked startled. "Caroline, what's the matter?"

Hearing who was on the phone, Sabrina rolled away from Nathan's side and covered her nudeness. She resented the intrusion.

"No better, huh? I'm sorry," Nathan went on. "Don't worry about Amber. She's fine. I've already made arrangements for her to stay with the Coopers when I have to work. I'm on the day shift for a while. So everything will be cool." He grew silent, listening. "Yeah...I'll be sure to tell her that," he said in a soft, caring voice.

He was silent after his conversation with Caroline. Sabrina resented the fact that Caroline had chosen this time to call and interrupt the swirl of wonderful moments they had created. She didn't want to know the details of their chat. She didn't want him to think she was envious. And she felt that the less she knew of Caroline's personal life the better.

She tossed back the covers. "It's getting late. I should be leaving. Heaven forbid if Amber awakens to find me here." She was disappointed to the flat ending of their evening.

"No, don't leave yet." He pulled her to him to form a spoon position. He kissed her shoulders and threw a leg over hers to keep her close. "I love you," he whispered into her ear.

When she heard those words, her heart lurched. He had said the words that she had yearned to hear. She twisted to face him and gazed into his eyes.

"I love you, Sabrina," he said again. There was a heart-rending tenderness in his eyes that matched his words.

She touched his face. "I...I love you, too, Nathan." She pressed her body to his and held him tightly.

Suddenly, there was a rapping on the bedroom door. "Daddy. Daddy, open up." The doorknob rattled impatiently. "I'm scared."

"Go back to your room," Nathan called over Sabrina's shoulder. "Turn on the light in your room. I'll be there in a minute, sweetheart." He sighed in consternation. "Nightmares. I never should have allowed her to watch the "Wizard of Oz" alone. It's the witch thing that bothers her." He kissed Sabrina, then rolled away from her to slip into some pajama bottoms to check on Amber.

Sabrina slid to Nathan's side of the bed. She turned on her stomach to smell the manly scent of him on the sheets. Then she turned on her back. He loved her. She loved him. Simple enough, she thought. But with Caroline around with her problems and Amber's return to his life, she felt as though she was the other woman in a married man's life. Would she ever have the privacy to enjoy the kind of happiness and relationship she knew they could have with all these obstacles cleared away? There had to be a way to make it work, she mused, studying the flickering glow of the candles. She had fallen so deeply in love with Nathan that she didn't want to risk the chance of not knowing what happiness could be theirs.

Chapter Ten

Grace Lewis saw the coolly attractive blonde woman, wearing sunglasses, enter the Soul Food Inn with another white woman who was near her age. The March wind had caused their complexions to turn a rosy shade of pink. Although the two women took a seat in Clara's station, Grace insisted on waiting on them. She recognized the blonde as the woman who had pushed her way back into Sabrina's man's life. She wanted to tell the hussy a thing or two. But she knew it wasn't her place. Sabrina didn't need her interfering in her business.

"Welcome to the Soul Food Inn. Would you ladies like menus?" Grace said, greeting the women.

The blonde, Caroline, didn't bother to look at Grace. "Two coffees. Decaffeinated."

"Sure," Grace said in a controlled voice to mask her annoyance at the woman's rudeness. She went off to get their order. She noticed that the blonde looked troubled; she leaned anxiously toward her girlfriend, who sat across from her in the booth. Something was going on and Grace was going to find out what. She was glad that the busboy was late. After she had served the women their beverages, she set to work clearing away the breakfast-shift dishes from the tables around the customers. She would clear away the tables behind them very thoroughly to hear what was going on.

"Another child is not what I was planning on," Caroline told her friend. "He's not going to like this when I give him the news. I'd told him I was on birth control."

"And just when do you plan on telling him?"

"I don't know. I'm not that far along. I'm trying to decide whether to keep it." She sipped on the coffee that Grace had given her. "This will ruin things. The last thing I want him to feel is that I'm trying to trap him."

A baby? Obviously Nathan had gotten those old feelings for his ex and had slept with her to see if there were still any sparks between them, Grace mused. Her lips puckered with annoyance. She knew that Sabrina and Nathan had had some trouble because of his family's intrusion on his life. Grace knew Sabrina: she had probably shut Nathan out physically until he could convince her she was the only one. And when she'd done that, he had probably crawled into his ex-wife's bed for physical satisfaction. That's what men did. At least that was the way Grace's men had treated her through the years.

Once the women were done with their coffee, they left.

Grace touched the ring that her daughter had given her for her birthday. Her heart turned over with the love she hadn't been able to express openly through the years. She decided to give Sabrina a call. She didn't want her baby to be hurt by the trap this sneaky woman was about to set for Nathan, Sabrina's man.

Sabrina was at Romantic Poses, going over notes to the speech she was to give at her old high school, John F. Kennedy. She had been invited by Kathy's husband to be part of Career Day. Nathan had been invited also. There were few black officers in Hunter's Creek. He was going to show up in his uniform and speak about the law and how the kids needn't always feel threatened by presence of police.

Sabrina was nervous about her speech. She hadn't been back to school since she'd graduated. And when she was there, she hadn't been the best student. But she had been full of ambition, with a plan that had worked. This was what she intended to emphasize in her speech. Most speakers encouraged kids to go to college. And this was a great idea for those who had the potential and the money. But there were those who could be just as successful with a chosen vocation that they could turn into a lucrative business and even a corporation. She wanted to give the average student a sense of hope that they could have a future other than a minimum-wage job waiting for them.

Sabrina pulled out her compact and studied her face. She needed a touch of lip gloss. She had done her hair that morning and put it up. She had chosen a rose-colored suit and a white shirt with a pointed collar, which she wore outside the collar of her suit.

The telephone rang. "Romantic Poses, where glamour lives," she answered in her quiet, professional tone.

"Sabrina, that woman just left here." It was Grace, her mother. She spoke in an angry frenzy.

"And how are you?" Sabrina said, not wishing to be pulled into gossip at this moment. She wanted to get her thoughts together for her presentation at the high school.

"Fine. Fine," snapped Grace. "Listen, I'm calling to give you some information you need to know about that woman who lives with your man."

"Caroline? Is that who you're talking about?"

"Yeah, that white woman. Her snooty behind came in here with a friend. They had decaffeinated coffee..."

"Mom, I don't have time for this. I have that thing at the high school."

"Sabrina, she says she's pregnant. I heard her confiding in her friend."

Dread and shock assailed Sabrina. Before she could respond, she tried to force her swirl of emotions into order. She placed a quivering hand on her chest and exhaled to calm her nerves.

"Sabrina, are you still there, baby?" Grace's voice was full of concern. "I should have come to see you to give you this news."

"Wh-what do you think this has to do with me?"

"C'mon, girl. Think. She and he have been alone in that house. You know they've probably gotten together for old time's sake. What man do you know is going to turn down-"

"I don't want to hear any more. You shouldn't be talking about this. You don't have any facts," Sabrina said haughtily.

"Okay, don't listen to me. Go to your man. Ask him about all of this. You should get it straight. I'd hate to see you get caught up in the middle of this mess. You've been far too patient with him and that woman living at his house anyway," Grace chided.

"I have to go." She cut off her mother's lecture. "I'll talk with you later."

"Get it straight, girl," her mother said before they said good-bye.

Sabrina sat at her desk, clutched her hands and lowered her head. She had been with Nathan the night before. He had come to her place. They'd relaxed, watching rented movies, and then made sweet, tender love. He had held her and kissed her and made her feel as though she was the center of his world. They had never talked about Caroline or the problems that kept her from moving out of his house and getting on with her life. She had come to Nathan's place in February and the month of March was just about over. According to Nathan, the only thing he and Caroline had in common was Amber. Was that really so? Had they given in to lust once or twice? Working in her beauty salon, the Raving Beauty, Sabrina had often heard women speak about giving in sexually to their ex-husbands in order to fulfill their own as well as their man's sexual appetites for the moment. According to the women, love had nothing to do with this behavior. Had this been the case? she wondered. Had such a casual liaison resulted in an unwanted pregnancy?

Gnawing on her lip petulantly, Sabrina tried to quell the irritation and anger that were building within her. Here I go again, she mused bitterly. Another woman had seduced a man she'd come to love, to trust. Sabrina rose from her seat and gathered her notes for the conference. Her hands trembled.

The news of Caroline's pregnancy tore at her insides. Why would Nathan keep this from her? she wondered. She sighed with resignation. She wasn't going to allow this conflict involving Caroline to eat away at her confidence. She wanted to make a good impression. And she was even though she was fiery mad at Nathan.

Nathan was late for the Career Day assembly. He arrived while a student was introducing Sabrina. He learned more of Sabrina's personal life than he'd had time to learn in their whirlwind romance. With the reappearance of Caroline and Amber, he'd spent what little time he had available with Sabrina, just convincing her that he wanted and needed her. The young female student spoke glowingly of Sabrina's businesses. She had been featured in many black business publications as a young black woman to watch.

When Sabrina took the stage to speak, she was a vision of delight. Her rose-colored outfit set off her complexion beautifully. Staring at her, Nathan was reminded of the sultry quality of the actress Dorothy Dandridge in the black movie classic, *Carmen Jones*. Whenever Nathan was near Sabrina, the lust in him was triggered.

Sabrina smiled with delight at her young audience and proceeded to deliver her motivational speech. She revealed to the students that she had been raised by a single mother who had worked as a waitress and as a maid for the motels in the area. As a teen, Sabrina had worked in fast food restaurants and, during the summers, she'd worked two jobs. She told them that she'd saved her money and never spent money foolishly. She'd bought her clothes at thrift stores and still managed to look decent. During Black History Month, she had been given the school assignment of doing a report on Madame C. J. Walker. Researching the bright and successful black woman's life, Sabrina had learned that Madame Walker had grown up poor. However, she had managed to build a successful career by developing black hair-care products and opening hair salons. Madame Walker managed to distribute her products throughout the country during a time when such businesses were unheard of. The life of this woman had inspired Sabrina. As a teen, Sabrina had had no idea what she was going to do with her life. She hadn't been the best student in the world. But she always put forth her best effort and she didn't mind working hard and saving her money. It was at that point that she had signed up for Cosmetology and attended the public school vocational program, where she was able to receive her training and get her beautician's license. She was grateful for the opportunity that the public school had given her. She told the kids that they must take advantage of the opportunities, as she had. She encouraged the students, male and female, to focus on a dream or have a plan for life, and make every effort to reach their goals.

She was given a roaring round of applause. She had been graceful and personable. There was no doubt in Nathan's mind that she had impressed a few kids enough to encourage them to seek their way to a bright future.

When Sabrina had seen Nathan slipping through the back door of the auditorium, her heart had burst with warmth. But her joy had turned to dismay as her mind had wandered to the information her mother had thrust upon her. She had turned her attention away from Nathan and tried to put her mind on her speech. She'd deal with her reawakened distrust of him later.

Yet the moment she'd taken the podium, she had been mindful of his presence. Despite her fresh doubts concerning him, it was comforting to have him there. His love and his nearness always filled her with a sense of security she hadn't known before. Every now and then she would steal a glance in his direction and notice the look of admiration upon his handsome face while she spoke. He looked so innocent. But he was the devil in disguise. After what she had learned, she realized that their love was doomed because of his betrayal with Caroline.

Once Sabrina had completed her speech, Nathan was introduced by a young man who was president of the student government. He made mention of the fact that Officer Atkins had been born in Hunter's Creek and left town with his family when he was a boy. He had chosen to return to the area because it was the birthplace of his father. His father had been a member of the police force, and Officer Atkins was following in his late father's footsteps.

If Sabrina hadn't received that informing phone call from her mother, she would have been impressed by what she heard about Nathan. But how could she be fascinated by a man who was two-faced and a liar? Livid, she had turned a deaf ear to his speech.

Nathan ended his address by telling the students who had come from at-risk neighborhoods, which he patrolled daily, that they must not let their circumstances define them. They might come from homes that were far from idyllic and fraught with grim situations, but it was no excuse for them to continue that cycle. He challenged them to want more and to strive higher.

After the speeches, the kids who were part of the program that Sabrina and Nathan mentored gathered around them to hug or shake hands. They wanted their classmates to know that they were friends with the two cool black people who had spoken.

Sabrina chatted with the kids from the Center. She smiled and made every effort to be pleasant with them. Nathan had approached her at the reception but she favored him with no smiles or easy conversation. She had been downright cool to him at the reception. Nathan was puzzled by her behavior. He could hardly wait for everything to be over so that he could have a chance to question her.

Nathan waited outside in the hall near the library where the reception was being held. The last of a group teachers, who were the sponsors of the program, chatted with Sabrina until she finally said good-bye. Nathan smiled, preparing to greet Sabrina alone at last.

Strolling out of the library, Sabrina met Nathan's warm expression with a cold stare. She didn't waste time stopping to chat. She kept strolling away from him, heading for the exit.

"Sabrina, what's the matter with you?" Nathan asked, falling into step with her.

"Do you really care about me or my feelings?" She glowered at him. She had reached the front exit and shoved opened the door to burst through it ahead of him, to get away from him.

Nathan trailed behind her as she strutted for the parking lot. He grabbed her by the hand to get her attention. "Talk to me. Explain why you're being so rude to me." He regarded her quizzically.

She halted, snatched her hand out of his. "How long were you planning on keeping your secret?" She narrowed her eyes with contempt.

A slight look of hesitation appeared in his eyes.

His idiotic behavior aggravated her. "Don't play dumb now. I've heard that Caroline is pregnant," she said bluntly. She whirled away from him and marched away toward her car.

"Sabrina! Wait!" Nathan called, catching up to her just as she reached her car.

She shot him an impatient look. "What can you tell me, Nathan? That it's not true? That the child she's carrying is not yours?"

A little tic worked on the side of Nathan's mouth.

Observing his reaction, she knew he was trying to come up with some kind of lie to appease her, to keep her hanging on.

"If you love me, you're going to have to trust me. I can't talk about it now. It has nothing to do with you or me," he said sharply.

Sabrina's eyes flashed with anger, her temples pounded thickly, and her throat grew tight. "You're wrong. It has everything to do with me and my pride, my self-respect.

Caroline is living with you. What do you think everyone in town will think when she starts to show? The first thing that crosses my mind is that the baby could very well be yours. Remember, I've seen the way she waltzes into your bedroom like she is still your wife," she said sardonically.

He shook his head ruefully. "When are you going to trust me? Why must I always be on the defensive over Caroline?"

Sabrina was so angry that tears had sprung to her eyes, and that made her angrier still. "You just don't get it, do you? I refuse to have this conversation any longer," she snapped. She proceeded to open her car and slide behind the wheel. She slammed her door, placing her key in the ignition.

Nathan leaned down to peer into her face. "What will I have to do or say to keep you from feeling insecure?" He glared at her with annoyance.

Sabrina gave him a scorching look. "I'm not insecure. I just refuse to allow you make me a laughing stock right here in Hunter's Creek."

"I don't care what other people think. You're the one who's concerned about images. As long as I know I'm doing the right thing, I don't care what people think of me." He straightened, hooked his fingers in his belt and assumed a confrontational stance. "Listen, I don't want to argue with you. Yes, she is pregnant. It's one of the reasons why she showed up in town. The father of her child is not ready to deal with Amber. He's white. He has sort of backed away from Caroline because he has learned Amber is biracial."

Clutching her steering wheel, Sabrina stared at him and raised an eyebrow in a questioning slant. "But surely he knew about Amber when he was dating Caroline."

Nathan's face twisted in anguish. "He didn't. You see, Caroline has hidden Amber away from her white peers. And especially this guy until right before she and Amber came here. It was the reason why she came to me. She had no one else to turn to."

Nathan's story of Caroline was sad. He had obviously made up his mind to support Caroline. It was an admirable gesture. However, Sabrina decided she had had enough of the whole drama and the web of problems their interracial marriage had created.

School bells chimed, signaling the end of the school day. Big orange buses rolled past them to the entrance of the building. The students began to spill from the building. Soon Nathan and Sabrina were surrounded by the loud chatter and laughter of the high school teens.

She gave Nathan a look of surrender. "I have had it Goodbye, Nathan. Good luck." Sabrina started her car, drove slowly off away from him on the graveled lot.

Nathan trotted beside her. "Sabrina, please...don't..." His voice sounded tortured.

She wouldn't look his way. She wasn't going to let him get to her. She kept driving, leaving him behind. Despair consumed her. A gentle rain had begun to fall. Sabrina studied the gray, somber skies. Her spirits matched the gloomy day. Her eyes misted. And one more time she felt loneliness fill her heart-where love had been.

$$\mathcal{C}hapter\ \mathcal{E}leven$$

"Grace, do you really think this is a good idea?" Malcolm asked, sitting in the Soul Food Inn. He stared up at the woman who served him southern-style chicken smothered in gravy and a side order of greens and yams—all on the house. "Sabrina isn't going to like the idea of you setting her up this way."

"I don't care. I know what she needs. Here it is spring and she does nothing but work night and day," Grace said. Her brow was furrowed with concern. "A young, healthy, attractive woman like herself needs a man in her life."

"But what about that police officer?" Malcolm asked. His dark complexion beamed with curiosity and a little malice.

"That's over with. Good riddance!" Grace grabbed Malcolm's shoulder and squeezed it. "Sabrina needs a genuine black man like you. When I saw you coming in today, I knew you were the answer to my prayers. I'd thought about you, but I didn't know how to get in touch with you since you've become a hot-shot celebrity." Grace grinned at Malcolm and winked. "Enjoy that plate of food. She should be here any minute." Grace thought of how she had had to persuade Sabrina to leave Romantic Poses for just a few minutes. "I made up some story about needing her to look at some papers for a new health plan I was intending to take out."

"Shame on you for being so deceptive." He brushed his mustache with his forefinger and thumb and smiled in pleasure at her.

"If anyone knows anything of being deceptive, it's you. Had you been faithful to my daughter, she wouldn't have gotten tangled up with that Nathan mess."

Malcolm cleared his throat and took a sip from his iced tea.

He was embarrassed that Grace knew the details of his indiscretion.

Grace glanced at the door. "Here she comes. Remember. This is your last chance. You've got to make her see that you and she belong together." She rushed away from Malcolm, whom she had sat in a side booth to greet Sabrina. "Sabrina, come take a seat at the counter. Let me fix you a cool beverage. Spring has come in with a blast. The weatherman says it's eighty-nine degrees."

Though the weather was unseasonably warm, Sabrina felt cool dressed in a matching beige blouse and slacks. She stared curiously at her mother; the woman seemed to be edgy. When she had received her mother's urgent phone call to come right over for a few minutes, Sabrina had been puzzled. Her mother never asked her advice about much. She had always done things the way she wanted to.

Grace slid a glass of tea with a slice of lemon in front of Sabrina. "Heard anything from that Nathan?" Grace asked casually.

"No, I haven't. And why should I?" Sabrina said without revealing any emotions. Yet the mere mention of Nathan's name caused a yearning within her.

"You know, I saw him the other night in the supermarket with that little bossy daughter of his. She was working his last nerve, too." Grace laughed. "The man looked as though he was at his wit's end, trying to calm her whining over some kind of cereal she wanted."

Sabrina stared down into her glass and pretended that she wasn't interested in what her mother related to her. "Where are the papers you wanted me to look over for you? And why are you changing health plans?" Sabrina scowled impatiently.

"They're in the back in the employees' lounge. Let me serve these customers who just came in and I'll go get them."

Sabrina's gaze followed her mother as she greeted the couple who took a seat in front of the restaurant. Her mother was up to something. *She must need money...a large sum of money.* Grace was probably trying to work up the nerve to hit her up,

Sabrina thought. She was generous with her mother, but no matter how much she gave her it was never enough. Her mother worked every day and made a decent salary, assisting the owner of the Soul Food Inn. But Sabrina also knew that her mother loved to gamble, loved to play the state lottery. She had found lottery slips lying around her mother's house, totaling up to fifty dollars for one day alone. She believed her mother had a secret competition going with her daughter. While Sabrina worked hard and invested her money in other businesses, seeking her fortune, her mother played the lottery. All it would take would be one set of lucky numbers to bring Grace enough wealth to exceed her daughter's arduous climb to success.

"Hey, lady." Malcolm climbed onto the stool next to Sabrina at the counter.

The heavy lashes that shadowed her cheeks in deep thought flew up at the sound of her ex-lover's voice. The scent of his familiar cologne tickled her nostrils. "What are you doing here?" Though she was annoyed by his unexpected appearance, she couldn't deny the fact that he looked great. It was obvious that life was good to him.

"Hunter's Creek is my home, too. I came for a few days to rest and recuperate." He twirled on the stool until his back rested against the counter and he could observe Sabrina's lovely face with ease. "Your mom gave me a warm welcome and a free plate of food. What are you going to offer me to show that you're glad that I'm here?" He smiled, challenging her for affection.

"All I can offer are words of hospitality. It's good to see you looking healthy and happy." She gave him half a smile.

In a quick once-over assessment, she studied his expensive shirt and designer jeans. A glittering gold chain adorned his neck and he wore an extravagant gold watch. Proof that Malcolm was on his feet and indeed doing very well with his career. Though she was happy for him, it wasn't enough to change her feelings for him. She didn't want him back in her life no matter how much acclaim he had received.

Looking over her shoulder for her mother, Sabrina noticed that Grace was making the rounds of the restaurant, which was slowly filling up. Her mother caught her watching her. She grinned a "gotcha" grin and turned her attention back to her customers.

It was then that Sabrina realized that her mother had conned her away from her work on this Friday afternoon in order to come to talk with Malcolm. She had been set-up and she didn't like it. Why was it her mother couldn't accept the fact that she meant it when she said she was through with Malcolm? Unlike her mother, who gave her errant male friends second and third chances to hurt her, Sabrina didn't play that game. She thought too much of herself to let anyone hurt her over and over again.

Sabrina fingered the sweat on her glass of iced tea. "Malcolm, I don't know what you and my mother have cooking. But whatever it is, I don't want any part of it. Grace has always been partial to you. As far as she's concerned, you can do no wrong." She sighed. "But then, she and I have never had the same values or taste when it came to choosing men."

Malcolm flinched. "Ouch! You sure aren't wasting words or time letting me know how you feel."

She glared at him. "Why can't you take me seriously? Is it that your ego won't allow you to accept the fact that there is one woman who doesn't live for the sight of you? I do not want you, Malcolm. Not now. Not ever," Sabrina said emphatically.

The good-natured expression on his face darkened. His mouth curved into a malicious grin. "Good-bye, Sabrina," he said sardonically. He bolted angrily from his seat and stormed out of the restaurant without even bothering to say anything to Grace.

Good riddance, Sabrina thought. She knew that her caustic words this time had cleared Malcolm out of her life for good. And as soon as her mother returned, she was going to reprimand her for trying to interfere in her life. Fuming with anger, Sabrina looked over her shoulder for her mother. She was anxious to set her straight for what she had attempted. The nerve of her mother, treating her as if she was a desperate spinster.

Sabrina glared in her mother's direction and saw an older man who had burst into the restaurant. He rushed up to Grace, waving his hands while he talked. More gossip, Sabrina surmised.

The usually friendly glow on Grace's face faded. Her brow creased with concern and she glanced over her shoulder at Sabrina.

The look that Grace gave Sabrina invoked a cold chill.

Clutching her order pad to her chest, Grace made her way to her daughter. "It's Nathan. He got caught in a crossfire during a robbery at the bank." She rested her hand on her daughter's back in a gesture of sympathy.

Sabrina felt as if a cold fist had closed over her heart; a sickening wave of terror knotted in her stomach. No, not Nathan. She straightened up, her head tilted back as if she had been hit by a bullet herself. He'd been rushed to the hospital, Grace related to her daughter, who had clamped her eyes shut.

Slowly, Sabrina moved off the stool and stumbled out of the Soul Food Inn and into the glare of the bright spring day. Her mother called after her, but she didn't respond. She kept walking as though she was oblivious to everyone. Her heart raced. Her throat ached until she allowed tears to spill from her eyes. *Nathan, I love you. Please, please don't die*, she thought, wiping away her unending tears with the heel of her hand.

Sabrina hopped into her car and raced straight for Hunter's Creek General Hospital. Frantic with worry over Nathan's condition, she dashed into the emergency room for information that would ease her worst fears. Much to her regret, she wasn't given any details concerning Nathan. Since she wasn't a member of his family, no word of his condition could be revealed to her, said the aloof receptionist. Sabrina glanced into the waiting area and saw Caroline. The woman sat with her arms wrapped around herself, looking as scared as Sabrina felt.

Sabrina approached the woman with whom she had exchanged few words in the last few months.

"I heard about Nathan. I'm sorry," Sabrina said, taking the seat next to Caroline. "How bad is he?" Her voice quivered with emotion.

Caroline stared at Sabrina coolly, but didn't offer any information.

Sabrina couldn't blame the woman for her aloof treatment toward her. Hadn't she treated her nearly the same way from the day she had met her and learned that Nathan had chosen a white woman as a wife, and had a child? Caroline looked vulnerable and scared. The sight of her made Sabrina feel ashamed for the way she had resented her. Suddenly it came clear to her what Nathan meant by empathy. This poor woman had been deserted by her family and had no one, other than sensitive, caring Nathan to turn to in her trouble. Sabrina rose from her seat to move to another, thinking that Caroline wanted nothing to do with her. And Sabrina knew she had given her many reasons to feel this way. She was consumed by her guilt.

Caroline reached out and snagged her by the wrist. "Wait! Don't go," she implored, sliding her hand down to Sabrina's fingers. "It doesn't look good." Her bottom lip trembled. Her face crumpled with sadness.

Sabrina gripped her hand and sat back down beside her. She draped her arm around the woman's shoulder, giving and seeking comfort for herself. Sabrina felt as though she couldn't bear the ordeal that had happened to such a good man. Caroline rested her head on Sabrina's shoulder and began to sob. And so did Sabrina. Though they were of different races, they were sisters, Sabrina realized. They both shared the same pain, devotion and respect for a wonderful man who had known all the time that love had no color.

In the next few hours after Nathan's shooting, the emergency room began to fill with people concerned over his condition. Several officers and a few of their wives showed up.

And there were people from his neighborhood who came over as soon as they heard it on the news. The teens from the Hubbard Community Center appeared, seeking out an unkempt and stressed Sabrina for answers and assurance that Mr. Nate would live.

The only word that Sabrina and Caroline had received was that Nathan had taken several bullets to his stomach and had lost a lot of blood. He had been in surgery for several hours.

When Sabrina saw her friend, Kathy Mason, enter the hospital, she rushed over to her. Sabrina fell into Kathy's arms and sobbed. She had worn a strong facade around the kids. But the moment she saw her friend she knew she could be herself.

"It's okay. Go on and cry, hon." Kathy held on to her friend and supplied her with tissues.

"I'm so scared. We haven't heard anything for awhile. Caroline called his brother and his mother."

Kathy steered Sabrina to a chair. "You've got to keep the faith. Nathan took good care of himself. He was in top physical condition, so all of that is on his side."

"I was awful to him. I was envious of the kindness he showed Caroline. I accused him of still being in love with her. I resented his daughter, Amber, for taking his attention from me just when I wanted it the most."

"Stop beating yourself up." Kathy took Sabrina's hand. "All of your resentment and jealousy was natural for a woman who had just found love with one of the most wonderful guys I know," she said in a soothing voice.

"No, it wasn't natural. The truth of the matter is that I was threatened by Caroline because she was white. I was afraid she was going to cast some kind of spell over him to make him not appreciate me. I feared that he would feel more of a man if he had the white, blonde and blue-eyed Caroline back in his life with their gorgeous daughter."

"I can understand your feelings. It's one shared by all black women. For some crazy reason, we feel that all black men are our property and that they have no right to look at anyone other than us for relationships. This has gone on since we were first brought to this country. It's a question of how a man can possibly fall for someone who is part of a group who, at one time, symbolized oppression for us."

Sabrina's ebony eyes were red-rimmed from crying and she had wiped away most of her make-up long ago. She felt unkempt and longed for a hot shower to invigorate herself. It was nearly seven o'clock in the evening. She looked around the waiting room at the people—black, white and Asian—who had come and gone in shifts to check on Nathan. They had come to see a man who happened to be black. A man who had-in one way or another-touched each one of their lives with some type of kindness or interest in them.

"Sabrina, how are you?"

Sabrina rose to her feet to greet Nathan's younger brother, Randall. They'd briefly met through Nathan at the Center in February. "I'm so sorry. I really am," Sabrina said, giving him a comforting hug.

"Oh, man, this is too much. My mother and I have spoken to his doctor. Nathan is in recovery. The next couple of hours will determine...well, you know." His eyes pooled with emotion.

An elderly woman came down the corridor and motioned to Randall. "Son, the doctors have informed me that there is a waiting room upstairs near the intensive care unit where you and I can wait. I want to be there whenever Nathan comes to."

"Mom, I'd like for you to meet a friend-a close friend of Nathan's. This is Sabrina Lewis. Sabrina, this is my mother, Bethany Atkins."

Sabrina smiled and extended her hand to the dark-complexioned woman with the kindly face and the curly, mixed gray and black hair. Mrs. Atkins was a bit taller than Sabrina's five-feet-four inch height and she wore a dress that reminded Sabrina of the kind of clothes teachers wore.

"Hello, dear." Mrs. Atkins managed a smile. "You're the young woman that Nathan was dating. He was supposed to bring you for a visit. Soon."

"Uh...yes, that's right." Sabrina didn't think the time was right for her to go into the details of how she and Nathan's relationship had fallen apart.

Mrs. Atkins patted Sabrina's cheek. "You look tired, baby. I appreciate your interest and you taking the time to be here. But as I told Caroline, who left to be with Amber and to get some rest, you should do the same thing. Randall will give you a call if there are any changes in Nathan's condition. He and I will be here through the night." She touched Sabrina's face again and smiled. "Hmm...you're such a pretty woman. Nathan told me how bright you are, too. That's quite a combination. I can see why he cares for you so much."

"Thank you," Sabrina answered softly.

"Come on, Randall. Let's get upstairs. We have to check on our boy and let him know we're here. The next time you hear from us, Sabrina, the news will be better. I've said my prayers. I have faith that He will see us through." She took her younger son's arm, walked to the elevator and disappeared inside.

"She right, you know," Kathy said, easing up beside Sabrina. "There's nothing else for you to do but wait. You can do that at home. Let's grab some take-out from somewhere and go to your house where you can relax and wait this thing out."

"He has his family. He doesn't need me, huh?" Sabrina's eyes grew misty. "After all, I stepped out of his life weeks ago." She met Kathy's concerned stare. "I love him. I drove him away." She broke into tears. "I...I hope nothing happens to him before I can let him know how much he really means to me."

Chapter Twelve

Two days after Nathan had been shot, he remained in intensive care. Only his family members had been allowed to see him. Since Sabrina couldn't see him, she'd either call the hospital or family to inquire of his condition. One night when Sabrina had fallen into a restless sleep, the phone rang, waking her from an intimate dream of Nathan and herself when they had been together and happy. She bolted upright in bed and blinked at the digital clock on her nightstand; it was six a.m.. She stared at the ringing phone, her heart racing. Was it bad news? Had Nathan taken a turn for the worse? Ridden with anxiety, she wanted to ignore the call. Suppose Nathan's condition had deteriorated or he had died? She stared at the phone as if it was a vile creature. She couldn't deal with such a reality. The phone rang persistently.

Finally, Sabrina gathered her courage to answer the phone. "Hello," she said reluctantly.

"Sabrina, this is Randall. Sorry to awaken you, but I couldn't resist calling you. I thought you'd like to know that...that Nathan is out of the woods. He is doing so much better. He's even been moved from intensive care. He's been asking for you."

Sabrina closed her eyes and covered her heart to quell her apprehension. She was overjoyed that Nathan was better and that he had asked for her. "I'm glad to hear that. I appreciate your call."

"Sabrina, he wants you to come visit him. Do you think you could come by sometime during the day? You'd be the perfect medicine for him."

"Oh Randall, that's sweet of you." Sabrina smiled. "But Nathan and I had separated and..."

"He hasn't said anything about that. All I know is he keeps asking about you. My mother told me to call you and to do what I could to get you over to the hospital."

"All right. Sure. I'll be there. I really would like to see him."

"Great," enthused Randall. "See you later."

Sabrina rolled out of bed, feeling a warm glow in her heart. Nathan wanted to see her. He had asked for her. She tried not to think in terms of reconciliation. This was definitely not the time for him to use his energy for a situation like that. The key thing was to keep his mind positive so that he could continue to recuperate.

Sabrina made her way into the kitchen. She was starving. She had had little to eat in the last few days, because she had been worried over Nathan's condition. She decided to prepare herself a hearty breakfast. When she saw Nathan, she wanted to look and feel in tip-top shape.

After eating a meal of scrambled eggs, bacon, and English muffins, Sabrina sat at her kitchen table, which looked out into her back yard at the colorful spring flowers that had begun to blossom. Spring was a time for growth-rebirth, she thought, finishing off a cup of tea. Could there be a change, a rebirth in her relationship with Nathan?

She noticed that the plants in her kitchen looked as limp and lifeless as she had felt—worrying over Nathan in the last few days—from the lack of attention she'd given them. She moved from her seat and proceeded to water and talk to the plants, sharing all her intimate thoughts of the past few days. Her task was interrupted by her doorbell. She glanced at her watch: nearly eight-thirty. She had no idea who would be visiting her at such an hour.

Still dressed in her long robe, she tightened the sash around her waist and ran her fingers through her hair to tame it. She hadn't combed it since she had gotten up for the day.

Out of curiosity, Sabrina glance through the tiny peek hole to see who was on the other side of the door. It was Caroline! Nathan's ex-wife. Sabrina couldn't imagine what would bring the woman there at such an hour. She hadn't spoken to Caroline since that awful day she had been at the hospital. She opened the door.

"Hi, how are you?" Sabrina asked in a gentle, welcoming tone. "Come on in." She held the door for the woman who had been like a thorn in her side until the other day in the emergency room.

"I'm glad I could catch you home. I know how busy you stay," Caroline said in a fragile tone. She followed Sabrina into her living room. "I bet I'm the last person you expected to visit you. But I have some things I'd like to talk with you about."

Sabrina took a seat on her sofa and invited Caroline to do the same. She imagined the woman needed a favor for herself or Amber. And Sabrina decided that she would oblige her. It would be what Nathan would want her to do.

Caroline's ivory face had a rosy flush and her blonde hair was combed away from her face in a tight pony-tail. Her blue eyes had a faraway look of distraction.

"Just what is it you'd like to talk about, Caroline?"

A weak smile trembled over the woman's lips before she finally spoke. "I'm leaving Hunter's Creek today. I want to be gone by the time Nathan leaves the hospital."

"Is that good for Amber to up and leave like this? I'm sure her father is going to need to have her around." Though Sabrina had wished a thousand times for Caroline and her daughter to disappear, she had had a change of heart about the situation. Nathan's crisis had erased her insecurity about his ex. Sabrina didn't want to see them leave while Nathan was still in the hospital. She knew how much Amber meant to him. Sabrina believed having his little girl around him would help put him back on his feet more quickly.

Caroline smoothed her hair nervously. "I'm not taking Amber with me. Nathan and I had a long talk before this nightmare occurred. I've chosen to give him sole custody of Amber."

"No! How can you give up your little girl?" Sabrina scowled. This time she wasn't speaking out of jealousy, but concern for Amber and what damage Caroline's choice could do to her.

"Don't look at me like that," Caroline snapped. "Don't judge me." She stood up, walked over to the picture window, and stared out pensively.

"I'm not judging you," Sabrina said impatiently, responding to Caroline's edginess. "Why have you come to tell me this? What does this have to do with me?"

Caroline turned and faced Sabrina. "He's in love with you. If you give him a chance, I believe you're going to be the next Mrs. Atkins."

Sabrina remained silent. She was thrilled. But she didn't believe it was right for her to flaunt her joy when Caroline seemed so distraught.

Caroline stumbled back to the chair and sat on the edge. "If you decide to get back with Nathan, I want you to look after my little girl. You're the kind of woman I'd like her to grow up to be."

Sabrina gave the woman a questioning look. "What are you talking about? You sound as though you're going away for good." She laughed nervously. The sight of tears welling in Caroline's blue eyes made her know that the woman was indeed troubled.

Caroline began to sob. "It's better for her. She might not understand it now, but it's best for her."

Sabrina sat on the arm of the chair beside her. How awful it must be for Caroline to give up Amber to get a second chance at happiness. Sabrina could see that Caroline was not a strong woman. She was a woman who needed to be pampered and taken care of.

Caroline stared up at her. "I'm pregnant. The man I love can't accept Amber. He knows that her father is a black man. He has aspirations of running for a political office and he doesn't want anything to hinder him. He loves me and I love him."

There it was, Sabrina thought, her reason for the visit. Sabrina was anxious to shift the responsibility of raising Amber to Nathan, so she could get back to the kind of life and world she was comfortable in. Her sudden appearance in Nathan's life had been a selfish move. Caroline had been waiting for the right moment to dump Amber on him without coming off looking like a villain.

Sabrina was incredulous at what she had heard. "How can you love a man who can't accept your child?"

Caroline's tears stopped. She stood and walked to the other side of the room. "Obviously, Nathan didn't tell you about my family or my friends," she said defensively.

"To be honest with you, I wasn't really that interested in you," Sabrina said bluntly.

"I saw that the moment I met you. You gave me that awful look that most black women gave me whenever they saw Nathan and me together. When Nathan and I first met and became involved, it didn't matter to me what people thought. It was exciting. You see, I come from a very conservative family, blue blood. My first memories were of my parents chiding me about my behavior, my friends. They constantly worried over what other people thought. Everything was about appearances. My father is head of a big corporation. He had sent me away to a college that his mother had attended. I didn't do very well. I left and went to live on my own to prove to my parents that I could take care of myself. I met sweet Nathan and the next thing I knew I was pregnant. My father was furious when he learned this. He told me to stay away from the family. They wanted nothing to do with me. I had tainted their family by marrying a black man and having his child."

Sabrina felt sorry for Caroline, who had been ostracized by her loved ones, her own flesh and blood. Sabrina saw tears spilling from her eyes and handed her tissues from the table nearby.

"I love my father and my mother. Just like Amber, I always strived to be Daddy's princess. I thought that they would love me no matter what. But I soon learned there were boundaries. I'd overstepped them." She heaved a sigh and clutched her heart as if she was easing her pain. "I loved Nathan, but I wanted my family's approval. I was destroyed when they wouldn't accept my phone calls, my letters. Even Christmas and birthday cards were returned to me unopened."

"They simply refused to accept your marriage," Sabrina said sympathetically.

Caroline nodded and made a pained expression. "I began to resent Nathan. I dreaded going out and being seen with him. I went a little insane. It caused me to question my feelings for him. I had an affair and he learned of it. Our marriage was over. I was sure that my divorce would cause my parents to welcome me back into the family. But there was Amber. A reminder to them of my 'mistake.' Sabrina, they wouldn't open their hearts to her—an innocent child. And what's worse, the people I usually associate with treat her no better. I can't bring her up in a world where she is made to feel unwanted. I've thought about this long and hard. It's best that she is with her father. He can give her what she needs. And I'm sure that you will help him."

"Hold on, Caroline. I'm sorry about all you've been through and what you're facing. But I haven't talked to Nathan. I'm not sure he's going to want marriage."

"Oh, he does! Trust me on this," Caroline assured her. "I'm going to have this child. I'm going to marry the baby's father. My parents will be able to live with my choice. And I'll be my father's princess again. He'll be pleased with my new life," she said as if she were trying to convince herself. She smiled nervously.

Sabrina pitied the woman who was emotionally torn by a situation she wasn't capable of handling. Caroline was clueless to the harm she would do her daughter by leaving her behind. Nathan was a good, strong man. There was no doubt in Sabrina's mind that he would be a great father to Amber. But he could never give his little girl what a woman, a mother, could.

"Please look after Amber. Don't turn her against me," Caroline implored.

"You're talking to the wrong person. Maybe you should talk to Nathan's mother or his brother, Caroline."

"No! I've come to the right person. I'm counting on you. I must leave. I have a plane to catch in a few hours. I've discussed this with Nathan's mother. She has agreed to look after Amber until...until you and Nathan get together." She rose from her seat with tears in her eyes and quietly left the house.

Sabrina didn't bother to go after Caroline. The woman had made up her mind and it would have been a waste of energy to make her see differently. She sat in her living room, thinking over what Caroline had asked of her. Was she capable of loving and caring for Amber as though she were her own? And most importantly, would Amber be willing to accept her love and to share Nathan with her?

She moved from the chair and walked toward her bedroom to get dressed. Nathan was waiting to see her. And Amber's fate with her would be based upon how she and Nathan would come to terms with all they had been through.

On her drive to the hospital, Sabrina thought about the awful name she had spewed at Nathan the night she had had too much to drink. "Crossover Brother." But he truly was a "Crossover Brother." Tears of shame stung her eyes. Nathan had crossed over all kinds of hurdles and prejudices. He worked at the Center and had helped troubled and lonely teens to cross over their consuming anger, inner turmoils, and shortcomings to become better individuals. And he had most definitely crossed over into her self-absorbed heart, her mind, and her soul, and showed her what real love could accomplish.

Arriving at the hospital, she met Randall and his mother standing in the hallway outside of Nathan's room.

"You made it." Bethany Atkins smiled. Her eyes sparkled with delight at the sight of the lovely woman. "It's good to see you under pleasanter conditions."

"It's really been a difficult time." Sabrina returned the woman's handshake. "My prayers and my thoughts have been with you."

"Thank you. Everyone in Hunter's Creek has been so wonderful to us. Nathan has made plenty of friends since he moved here. But I'm not surprised. He's always been the kind of person that people want to be around. He's like his father. Now there was a charmer." She chuckled.

"Pops was the man," Randall agreed. "Though he's gone, he still has friends and co-workers who kept a watchful eye out for Nathan and me after he passed. They made sure that we became the kind of men our father wanted us to be. It's like having guardian angels all over the place."

"Be thankful that you are loved," Randall's mother said, taking his hand. "That's a precious gift. Your father knew it. Nathan knows it, and I believe you're learning, too."

Bethany smiled at Randall, then turned her attention to Sabrina. "He's waiting for you. We were leaving. We have to get home. Amber will be getting out of school soon. I promised her I'd be at the bus stop, waiting. I hope to see you later, Sabrina."

Sabrina imagined the woman was disappointed at Caroline for deserting her grandchild. But she was certain that this woman, who had raised two teenaged boys on her own, would see to it that Amber lacked for nothing that was truly important to her. Like love.

Sabrina stared at the door of room three seventy-three. She hoped that the moment Nathan saw her he would see that she was still in love with him. She fumbled at the waistband of her slacks to make sure that her blouse was tucked in properly, and took a deep breath to relieve the tension she felt. Reluctantly, she pushed at the door and then halted, anxiety coursing through her. For a moment, she wondered if Nathan really did want to see her. Or was this all a ploy of Randall's to bring them together? She would feel ridiculous if she did not find that Nathan wanted her back. With bated breath she entered his room. She found him resting comfortably in bed. His face was turned toward the window, washed with the beauty of the sunny day.

"Nathan," Sabrina called softly.

Slowly, he rolled his head on the pillow in the direction of her voice. He blinked a couple of times as though he thought he was dreaming. A smile tilted the corners of his mouth. He lifted his arm and held out his hand.

Sabrina dashed over to him and accepted it.

He pulled her toward him, kissed her tenderly and held her. "Sabrina, my angel, my love."

Tears spilled from her eyes and she pressed her face next to his. "I love you. I love you. I was so afraid that I wouldn't have the chance to say that to you." She leaned away from him to look into his marvelous eyes and drink in his wonderful features. Though his caramel complexion was still somewhat pale, she thought he looked great. He was alive and on his way to recovery. And best of all, he wanted her.

He grabbed the control for his bed and pressed the button to raise his head. He insisted that she sit on the bed beside him.

"Sabrina, I have something for you." He retrieved a small, blue velvet box from under the covers and handed it to her.

Easing open the box, she found a diamond ring. A cry of joy broke from her lips.

"Will you marry me, Sabrina?" he asked, watching her with tears glistening in his eyes.

"Oh yes! Yes!" She lavished kisses on his face.

He laughed and winced at the same time. The stitches he'd received from surgery pained him. "Let me put that ring on your finger," he ordered good-naturedly.

Sabrina handed him the box and held out her left hand to him.

He slid it on her finger, then kissed her fingertips. "You have all my love for life," he vowed softly.

Before Sabrina could respond, a nurse entered the room, carrying a lovely bouquet of red roses.

"You rang, sir," the nurse said in a playful tone. "Officer Atkins, here is your order as you requested." She grinned like a Cheshire cat at Sabrina and held out the flowers. "You're a lucky woman."

Sabrina beamed at the added token of flowers. Tears of joy blurred her vision.

Nathan's face glowed, witnessing her gratitude for the roses. He tucked the sight of her loveliness in his heart and mind to savor whenever he wanted. "Take the flowers, sweetheart. The nurse is a busy woman who has taken the time to play Cupid for me," he said. He laughed carefully, holding his surgical area.

Accepting the flowers, Sabrina felt blissfully happy, fully alive. She sniffed their fragrance and caressed the blossoms against her cheek.

"And to think I came here to cheer you." She grinned.

"Randall helped to pull this off. He's been rooting for us all along," Nathan said, taking her hand.

"We're going to be so happy. You, me and Amber," she said enthusiastically.

When Sabrina mentioned his daughter's name, his mouth eased into a broad smile of satisfaction that lighted up his eyes. "Sit on this chair near the bed, so I'll be able to kiss you and feel your warmth." His voice was soft and full of the love he felt for her.

Sabrina did as he requested. She sat beside him, carefully rested her head on his shoulder and clutched her bouquet of beautiful flowers.

Nathan slipped his arm around her waist, gazing down at her radiant face. Leaning forward and struggling with his pain, he kissed her tenderly. Sabrina was indeed somebody special. And he felt as though he was the richest man in the world to be this very special somebody's someone.